Down by Law

D0012843

Also by Ni-Ni Simone

The Ni-Ni Girl Chronicles
Shortie Like Mine
If I Was Your Girl
A Girl Like Me
Teenage Love Affair
Upgrade U
No Boyz Allowed
True Story

Hollywood High series (with Amir Abrams)
Hollywood High
Get Ready for War
Put Your Diamonds Up
Lights, Love & Lip Gloss
Heels, Heartache & Headlines

Published by Kensington Publishing Corp.

Down by Law

NI-NI SIMONE

Dafina Books

KENSINGTON PUBLISHING CORP.
www.kensingtonbooks.com

To the extent that the image or images on the cover of this book depict a person or persons, such person or persons are merely models, and are not intended to portray any character or characters featured in the book.

DAFINA BOOKS are published by

Kensington Publishing Corp.
119 West 40th Street
New York, NY 10018

Copyright © 2015 by Ni-Ni Simone

All rights reserved. No part of this book may be reproduced in any form or by any means without the prior written consent of the Publisher, excepting brief quotes used in reviews.

All Kensington titles, imprints, and distributed lines are available at special quantity discounts for bulk purchases for sales promotion, premiums, fund-raising, and educational or institutional use.

Special book excerpts or customized printings can also be created to fit specific needs. For details, write or phone the office of the Kensington Sales Manager: Kensington Publishing Corp., 119 West 40th Street, New York, NY 10018. Attn. Sales Department. Phone: 1-800-221-2647.

Dafina and the Dafina logo Reg. U.S. Pat. & TM Off.

ISBN-13: 978-0-7582-8774-8
ISBN-10: 0-7582-8774-7
First Kensington Trade Paperback Printing: August 2015

eISBN-13: 978-0-7582-8775-5
eISBN-10: 0-7582-8775-5
First Kensington Electronic Edition: August 2015

10 9 8 7 6 5 4 3 2 1

Printed in the United States of America

Dedicated to Ke'Ron L. Green for staying with me on the phone until the wee hours of the morning. For believing in my story and encouraging me to just write without standing over my own shoulder. I thank you for that. Here's to you never hesitating and having only one request! I hope the pages make you smile.

Acknowledgments

Thanking the Creator for the gift of storytelling and the outlet to express it.

To my husband, my parents, my children, my entire family and friends: Thank you for your love and support.

Amir Abrams, thank you for being there whenever I needed you. You are truly the best!

K'wan Foye, thank you for only being a phone call away.

Sara Camilli, thank you for all of your hard work.

Selena James and the Kensington family, I truly appreciate every one of you for all that you do.

The bookstores, book clubs, schools, libraries, and everyone who has ever supported me in my career: I could never thank you enough!

And saving the best for last: the fans! I have the best fans in the world. You all inspire me in so many ways. I pray that *Down By Law* touches, teaches, and entertains!

Please email me at ninisimone@yahoo.com so that I may know what you think!

One Love,

Ni-Ni Simone

Let's go back in time...
waaaay back.

Brick City, 1985

No iPhones.

No iPods.

No CDs.

No Internet.

No cell phones.

Pimps had car phones.

Drug dealers had beepers.

The bigger your radio, the more respect you got.

Rap battles and mix tapes regulated if you had the juice or not.

Top rockin' it, windmills, and beatboxin' electrified the cardboard and the concrete.

Beat bitters and dope style takers were straight suckers.

Hip-hop was real.

Kool DJ Red Alert was on the attack, and Mr. Magic couldn't make him disappear.

Fab 5 Freddy was the underground mayor.

Jesse Jackson had hope and was so dope that he wanted to be president...twice.

Don Cornelius had soooooooooul.

Ronald Reagan crowned the welfare queen, while his wife, Nancy, wanted the subjects to just say no.

Crack was on a mission.

AIDS was dissin' and dismissin'.

And yo' rep was everything. Period.

1

The message

All I could do was get off the ground and run. No lookin' back.

No time to hook off on nobody.

Just zoom through the streets of Newark until I reached the corner of Muhammad Ali and Martin Luther King Boulevard and made a mad dash for Douglas Gardens. Better known as *Da Bricks*. Twenty L-shaped, seven-story buildings that took up four blocks, connected by a courtyard. To the right was a basketball hoop. No net. Just a rim. To the left was a row of ten rusted clotheslines, where the only thing that hung safely was a beat-up pair of white Converses.

There were begging-behind crackheads er'where, scratching they necks, carrying they snotty-nose babies on they hips. And dope fiends who stood up, nodded out, but never fell down.

There were some people leavin' out for work. And some just coming in; rushing straight from the bus stop to they apartment. Never speaking to nobody. Never looking no other way but straight. Never coming back outside until the next day.

Old ladies hung out the window and cussed out anybody making noise.

Winos sat on the stoops and complained about yesterday, every day.

Somebody's boom box echoed through the air. And another somebody was spittin' rhymes.

Kids raced behind the ice cream truck like roaches who'd seen the light.

Fresh ballers had a pot of money at their side while they rolled dice.

B-Boys break danced, making the cardboard come alive.

Then there was me. Twelve-year-old Isis. Five feet even. Short arms. Short legs. Skin the color of honey. A too-big booty bouncing. And size six feet zippin' er'thing, as I burst into building one-seventy-two, rushed up the pissy stairway, and swore that once I got inside, to apartment three-twenty-five, I was never gon' come back out. Ever.

"What da hell wrong witchu?" Daddy stood up and slammed both hands on the kitchen table as I clung to his waist and buried my head into his side. My mother, Queenie, and brother, Face, did they best to stop the guns, blades, and bricks of rock that lay on the glass table top from sliding to the floor.

"Isis. You hear me?" Daddy lifted my chin.

I didn't answer him. Instead, I wiped snot with the back of my bruised and trembling hand.

Queenie frowned. Shoved a hand up on her hip. "Ain't nuttin' wrong wit' this lil high yellow heifer." She snorted and popped her full lips. "'Cept she selfish as the day is long. Mannish. Spoiled. And she stay lookin' for a reason to tear up our groove and bust up our party. But I tell ya what: Had my rock hit the floor, or one of them guns went off, you was gon' have a reason for dem tears. Now tell us what happened to you!"

"Relax, Queenie," Daddy said sternly. "Now, baby girl—"

"Baby?" Queenie sucked her teeth. "This strumpet ain't no baby. When I was her age, I was ripe, ready, and on my own. Baby? Puhlease. Ain't no dang babies around here. Now, Isis, you heard what I said—"

"Pop! Queenie!" My fourteen-year-old brother, Montez—who we called Schooly 'cause Queenie said it didn't matter that he was a touch of retarded, he was still the smartest black man she knew—bolted into the room. "Yvette is at the door crying and saying some chicks jumped and jacked Isis for her Shell Toe Adidas and her dookie chain."

"And my neon jelly bracelets!" Yvette's quivering voice squeaked in from the hallway.

I could feel all eyes land on me.

Before I could decide what to do, Face stuffed a nine at his side.

"Sit down," Queenie said. "And put that gun back on the table."

"But Queenie," he pressed.

"What did I say?!"

He put the gun back and Queenie walked over to me. She slung me around, and my wet lashes kissed the base of her brown neck.

"You let some hos do what to you?" She shoved me into the corner and sank her elbow into my throat, pinning me against the wall. The heels of my bare feet was in the air and the tips of my toes just swept the floor.

My heart raced.

Rocks filled my mouth.

I couldn't breathe.

I couldn't think.

All I could do was suck up snot and do my best to not to choke on it.

Queenie pressed her elbow deeper into my throat, causin' me to gag. "Look at me when I'm talkin' to you! You out there in the street lettin' some hos disrespect you?"

I lifted my gaze to meet hers and spotted a gleamin' blade in her right hand. My eyes sprang wide and drops of piss drowned the seat of my panties.

I froze.

She leaned into my ear. *"I asked you a question."*

Silence.

"Answer me!"

"I can't...breathe...."

She eased the pressure of her elbow a little, just enough so that I could speak but not too much where I could move. I licked the salty tears that ran over my lips. My stomach bubbled and I knew at any moment Queenie's elbow would be speckled orange.

I hesitated. "They-they-they-they-they...snuck us. We was mindin' our business and they stole on me. All me and Yvette was doin' was walkin' down the street and some chicks came outta nowhere. I swear to *God*, Queenie, I didn't see 'em comin'."

"Who was it?"

My eyes shifted from hers to the floor. "I don't know." I shrugged. Then looked back at her.

Queenie eyed me from my torn neon-pink and stretched-neck T-shirt, to my skin-tight Jordache jeans. Her thin neck turned into a road map of thumping veins and her glare burned its way through me.

I chewed the corner of my bottom lip.

Queenie was going to kill me. Question was: when?

I glanced over at a boney and freckle-faced Schooly, whose sunken chestnut eyes revealed that he was petrified. He was nothing like our eighteen-year-old brother, Ezekiel Jr., who up until he saw the movie *Scarface* we'd called Lil Zeke. Now we had to call him Face.

Face would try anything once, including runnin' up on Queenie. But Schooly…Schooly was slow. A straight pussy. Always went to school. Never smoked weed. Never did no licks wit' us. Never got in no trouble. Never talked back. And with his twisted left leg that dragged, there was no way he was gon' leap over here and save me.

I looked toward the doorway. A teary-eyed Yvette stood peekin' into the kitchen. Another useless one.

Queenie snatched my face around. "As much as you stay fightin' in school and I have to cuss the teacher out. And as much as you 'round here tryna fly kick Face in the chest and he makes two of you, ain't no way you got robbed. You musta gave it to 'em."

"Nah-uhn," I spat, shaking my head. More tears filled my eyes. "They jacked us. At the store. Soon's we walked out the door. Knocked Yvette out cold. Slapped me to the ground and straight jacked me for er'thang. I was looking fresh to def too."

I scanned Queenie's eyes. They narrowed to icy green slits. She pointed the tip of the blade lightly into my jugular and I held my breath.

Hot specks of spit checkered my face as she said, "One thing I can't stand is somebody tryna play me. You must want me to slice your lil lyin' throat open and whip yo' fresh lil—"

"Okay. Okay. Just pleeeeeeeeease don't kill me. Pleeeeeeeease. Queenie. See ummm, what had happen was, ummm—I was in a break-dancin' battle—" My heart raced and my body dripped with sweat. Queenie hated break dancin'. "And the prize was a Doug E. Fresh cassette tape." And she hated cassette tapes. She was stuck on forty-fives and eight-tracks. "But I wanted that tape baaaaaad. So I killed it on the cardboard. And this girl Aiesha and her crew got mad 'cause I won."

"*And* . . ."

"I called 'em fake break-dancin' hos. I gave 'em the middle finger and told 'em to take they ugly behinds home. But. That didn't give 'em no reason to jack us!"

"*And* they was bigger than us!" Yvette tossed in. "*Waaaaaaay* bigger than us!"

"I know you ain't care about no size?!" Queenie snapped, grimacin' at me. "I know you ain't stand out there and let some ho beat you down 'cause she was big?!"

"No!" I practically shook my head off. "Size don't matter to me. 'Cause I woulda left they lungs on the sidewalk. But. It was four of them and only two of us. It wasn't a fair one, Queenie." Fresh tears sprang from my eyes. "Now I don't have nothin'. Not my favorite sneakers. Not my chain. And not my tape. How I'ma be fly *and* jacked? That's bad. Real bad. Hella bad."

"And where they jack you at?"

I sucked in a breath. Slowly eased it outta the side of my mouth. "We dipped off."

"Where?"

I hesitated. "Umm...we was in Weequahic—" Before I could finish, Queenie slapped me so hard that my neck whipped to the left and a gush of spit kicked its way through my lips.

She'd told me a million times to stay outta the park. That too many girls was raped and left floatin' face down in the lake. But...I was nowhere near the lake. The break-dancin' battles was always on the playground. I started to tell her that, but judging by the look on her face, I didn't think now would be a good time.

Besides, it was no secret that Queenie hated me. Before I came burstin' through her golden coochie, she'd been daddy's bottom treat, beatin' the concrete and keepin' his stable of hos tight just to prove her love. But. Once she gave birth to me, the hustle changed.

"A'ight. That's enough, Queenie," Daddy said, finally saving my life. "Get that blade outta my baby's face and don't slap her no more."

"Zeke—"

He shot her a look. The same look he'd given her the other night when he'd told her to shut up. She hadn't listened. So he'd wrapped his belt around her neck, dragged her around the room, and made her be quiet. "I *said* that's enough. Now come here, baby girl."

Queenie grabbed me by the shoulder and pushed me over to Daddy. He pulled me into his lap and wiped my face and neck with the palm of his hand. "Did you forget who you is?"

Silence.

"Answer me."

I blinked back tears and sniffed. "No. I ain't forget."

"Well, it's lookin' that way to me. You lettin' somebody punk you in the street."

"I ain't forget, Daddy."

"Then talk to me. Lay it down fo' me. Who is Isis Carter?"

I sucked up snot. "Yo' princess. Yo' baby girl, and I ain't never s'pose to be scared."

"And why is that?" Queenie interjected.

" 'Cause I'm betta than that."

"And . . . ?" Daddy pressed.

"I know my rep is er'thing. That's why I know how to shoot my own gun and fight my own fight—"

"Damn skippy." Queenie beamed.

Daddy continued, "Then you already know you gon' have to go back out there and handle this on ya own."

Silence.

"Now, go change them clothes and getchu a bat—"

"A bat? Oh, hell no. She gon' take this blade." Queenie placed the shiny metal in the palm of my hand.

My eyes bulged and my heart sank to my feet. I'd been in a whole lotta throwdowns, but this was a whole other level.

"This is war," Queenie spat. "So you may as well get your mind right. 'Cause you goin' back out there. And if you come back in here wit' out them tennis shoes, that gold chain, and that Doug E. Somebody tape, then I'ma peel the high yellah black offa you." She pointed to the pile of blades on the table. "Now try me if you want to."

2

Turntables might wobble, but they don't fall down

My life flashed before me. And my heart dropped through the black hole in my stomach and hid out there the whole bus ride. I kept clearing my throat and doing my all not to piss in my panties, but it seemed like er' two minutes a little bit would ease out. And then a few minutes later a little bit more piss would come through.

Yvette sat next to me and quietly chewed on the loose meat that framed her tore-up cuticles. I tried my best not to reach over and TKO her face for making me more nervous than I had to be. "Yvette! Dang! Would you cut it out?"

"Cut what out?"

"You know what. Acting like a punk. Where is your heart?"

She sucked in a breath. "At home. I'm scared."

"Scared? How whack is that? What, yo' panties too tight? You got on a training bra or somethin'? You better wake up and get your life together."

"Don't be questioning my life! And anyway, what about

you? 'Cause earlier when they jacked you, you pissed all in your pants. And don't say you didn't 'cause when you took off runnin' your whole ass was wet. And it's wet again." She pointed to my lap.

"Lies! This is sweat. I ain't neva pissed on myself! I was just nervous. Caught off guard. That's all! But now I got my mind right."

"I hope so. And I hope when you go to one-two Aiesha, you don't miss."

Chills pricked through me and I heaved at the thought. "Is you crazy? Don't be sayin' that! Don't be jinxin' me! I ain't gon' miss!"

"But Aiesha's hella big. She's like ten feet."

I sucked in a corner of my bottom lip and pulled in a vision of Aiesha. I could clearly see her, from her stacked blond bob to my sneakers on her feet. She wasn't exactly ten feet. More like nine. I rolled my eyes. "And? She *still* can't beat me. And anyway, it ain't about size. It's about heart."

"Is you really gon' cut her?"

I ran my tongue alongside the blade I had flush against my jaw. Truthfully: I was more comfortable with a gun. All I really knew how to do with a blade was talk without cuttin' up my cheeks. Queenie had taught me that. But I'd never thought about using one. Until now.

"Am I really gon' cut her? If she don't gimme back my stuff, I'ma slice her throat."

Yvette hesitated. "Maybe we should take it to her friends first."

"Beatin' down herbs ain't the move." I pointed into Yvette's lap at the padlock-filled sweat sock that Queenie had given her. "You better swing that thing at the head beast in charge. Plus. You already know Queenie gon' kill me if I come back home with nuffin'."

Yvette nodded. "Word."

"A'ight, then," I said, as the bus approached our stop. I inched out of my seat, reached up, and yanked the corded buzzer. A few seconds later the bus came to a complete halt. "Time to get off. Come on, Yvette." We walked out the bus's back door.

I did my all to brush off any feelings of nervousness that crept up on me as we walked into the park.

"There they go," Yvette whispered, pulling me behind the bushes.

I gasped, eased my head over the shrubs, and spotted Aiesha sitting on a swing: profiling my chain, rocking my Shell Toes, and sucking on a lollipop like she was a dime. And her two baldheaded friends each flossed in three of Yvette's jelly bracelets, like they bought 'em.

"This. Is. My. Jam." Aiesha hopped up and did the snake, her boom box blasting my tape. Her dumb posse laughed and, as if on cue, this whack tramp switched from the snake to the Alf dance.

I swallowed.

Yvette sniffed.

My stomach flipped.

Yvette groaned, "Issssssissssssssssss."

"You better shut up and straighten yo' back!" My heart raced and a sudden urge to piss threatened to drown the seat of my panties again.

Shake it off.

You got this.

We stepped out from behind the bushes and walked over to Aiesha. "Excuse you." I placed a hard right hand up on my hip, stabbed an index finger into the air, and sent a piercing look through her. "You need to be giving me back my stuff. Now!" I cocked my neck to the left and parked it there.

Aiesha's face lit up. She looked me over from head to toe, then fell out laughing. She laughed so hard that her body rocked and tears of joy fell from her eyes. "Ciara, Pam," she called out to her friends. "You see this?" She pointed to me and Yvette. "Somebody better get these lil girls 'fore they get they feelins hurt again and catch another beat down."

"Or before we jack 'em again." Pam laughed and pointed to my feet. "'Cause them lil purple kangaroos she got on is stupid fresh."

Aiesha agreed, "They is kinda dope."

My heart thumped and dropped to the bottom of my stomach. *Who is Isis Carter? Yo' rep is everything. You let some hos disrespect you? I'ma peel the high yellah black offa you.*

I cleared my throat. I hated these tricks. And I hated that they was laughin' at me.

Takin' me for a joke.

I ain't no joke.

And I wasn't gon' let these broke-down project skanks play me in the middle of the park for one. Otherwise, I'd never be able to show my face again. And I wasn't about to let that happen. Besides, if I went home empty handed I already knew Queenie was gon' slit my throat. And I'd scalp these bimbos before I let that go down.

It was all I could do not to piss on myself. I pressed my thighs tightly together and tried my best to fight off the edge. "I don't know wassup witchu and yo' pet alleyway-skeezers, but I ain't da one. Now, gimme back my stuff—"

"Or what?" Aiesha snapped. " 'Cause you ain't 'bout to do nothin'. Matter fact, take off them sneakers and gimme them two-tone Lees you got on too." She and her crew moved in closer to me and Yvette. I could hear Yvette stealing quick sips of air.

I swallowed and squeezed my thighs tighter. My stomach flipped, ached, and bubbled. But. I had to handle my bizness and let 'em know the worst mistake they *ever made* was comin' for me. 'Cause if I didn't, then er' punk and er' lil chickenhead lookin' for a come-up was gon' try and fly by effin' wit' me.

I had to put an end to that now.

Right now.

"You got me messed up!" I spat, hatin' myself 'cause my voice was tremblin'.

Aiesha and her crew roared in laughter, leavin' me and Yvette wit' no choice but to sneak 'em.

Whap!

Crack!

Bam!

Slice!

"AHHHHHHHHH!"

"Hold up, cuz!" some unknown dude said, skidding backwards across a plank of cardboard, getting away from me and Yvette. All the little kids scattered and er'body else stood back and watched.

Aiesha fell backwards to the ground. Her bloodcurdling screams shrieked through the air as her friends jetted outta the park, leaving her there.

"AHHHHHHHHH!" Aiesha continued to scream and ball up like a baby.

"Stank ho!" I kicked her in the head and then spit on her. "You better not never"—I took my chain from around her neck and snatched my sneakers off of her feet—"come for me again!"

"Ever!" Yvette swung her lock and sock, hitting Aiesha straight in the stomach. Then she yanked Aiesha's smashed bamboo earrings outta her ears and roughly wrestled the four-finger name ring from her hand. Once Yvette secured her goods, she said, "Isis! Your tape."

I smiled in admiration that Yvette was putting it down and making sure I didn't forget a thing. "No," I said. "I'm not gon' just take the tape. I'ma take the boom box too!"

And once we got all of our stuff and half of Aiesha's, I hit her in the head with one last kick. "Trick!"

3

Eight million stories

Me and Yvette was on top of the world.
Officially thorough.

After we showed Queenie that we'd gotten all my stuff back, plus some more, she told us she was proud and that now our rep was clear: You come for us. We come back even harder for you. Fair exchange. No robberies.

I closed my bedroom door, lit some Black Love incense, and then placed the boom box we took from Aiesha on my bedroom window sill. Afterwards, I pushed play on my tape and turned the volume up. All the way up, 'til the bass made my Super Nature and Whodini posters shake.

"This radio is bangin'!" I said as I did the wop and flopped across my bed.

"Yop. But I betchu it ain't fresher than this." Yvette smacked her lips, cocking her neck from one side to the other, showing off Aiesha's earrings and her four-finger name ring.

I reached in my nightstand drawer, took out a pack of

E-Z Wider and a bag of weed. "Only thing is: that ain't yo' name on the ring." I emptied the bag of weed onto the back of my Kurtis Blow album cover.

Yvette shrugged. "So. I'ma still rock it...unless you think she gon' run to five-oh and I should throw it away?"

I shuddered. Shook chills off. Aiesha snitchin' had never crossed my mind until now. "I don't think she gon' do that. But if she does: first was a slice to the face. Next stop is the throat."

Yvette took the E-Z Wider, rolled a joint, and licked it close. "You left her jaw wide open though. She might drop dime on you for that." She sparked up and took two pulls.

"If she tells on me," I said as Yvette passed me the joint, "best believe she gon' tell on you too. And I ain't afraid of doin' time. What about you?" I blew a slow and steady cloud of smoke toward the ceiling and waited for the lie I knew Yvette was 'bout to tell.

"Scared? What is that? I handle mines at all times. You seen my work."

"Umm-hmm. Yeah, I seen it. You shakin' frames up."

I passed Yvette the joint and she took a pull. I could tell by the way she rocked her head and her eyes hung half mast that she was feelin' good. "Isis, can you show me how the game go again? Please."

"What game?" I reached in my drawer and pulled out a brown paper bag full of candy and Crunchy Cheez Doodles.

"You know what game. The pimp game." She mashed the joint in the ashtray.

I tossed a cheese doodle in my mouth. "Daaaaaaaaaaang. Why you always sweatin' that?"

"'Cause I'ma be a pimp just like Mr. Zeke. I'ma be hella

rich. You seen how fly y'all apartment is? Mph. I want some of this. Now come on. *Please* show me."

I rolled my eyes to the ceiling, stared at my New Edition poster for a quick minute and then locked eyes with Yvette. "First of all and forevermore, I keep telling you that a broad can't be no pimp. She can only be the ho, which is why you need to dream up another hustle."

"That ain't true! My teacher, Ms. Mansfield, said a woman can be anything she wanna be!"

"Ms. Mansfield is stupid. She the same one be around here buying crack from my daddy. That's why y'all always got a substitute, 'cause she stay high. In a minute he gon' have her beatin' that concrete. Trust me."

Yvette sucked her teeth. She loved that chickenhead teacher of hers. "Whatever. You gon' show me or not?"

"Okay. I'ma show you. But only 'cause you my home-girl." I jumped off the bed. "Let's say you a pimp and you spot a new chick in town. She just got off the Greyhound."

"The Greyhound? Why would a pimp be at the bus station? Er'body know they rollin' in Cadillacs." Yvette reached in my candy bag and pulled out a pack of Pop Rocks.

"No. What er'body know is that a pimp gotta go where the weak broads go 'cause they the easiest to turn out. The bus station is where my daddy got Queenie from."

"For real?"

"Yeah. Queenie ain't from around here. She from Down South. Norfolk. Now, could you be quiet and let me talk?" I huffed. "Now back to the bus station. So let's say you spot fresh meat. And as a pimp, it's yo' job to know that all hos is runnin' from somethin'. Might be a mama who threw her out. A daddy, her mama's man, her uncle, brother, cousin, or a granddaddy. And probably one or all of 'em can't keep they hands offa her. Or maybe she just got outta prison and don't have nobody. Could be eight million different stories. But now, if I'ma fly pimp, then I'ma set it up where I accidentally bump into you. And then I'ma say, 'Ah 'scuse me, sweetness. I didn't see all this greatness.' "

Yvette's bloodshot eyes danced in delight and her mouth fell open.

I continued, "And the ho gon' smile just like you smilin' 'cause ain't nobody never told her she was great befo'. And when she smiles, that's your cue to keep on talkin'."

"So whatchu s'pose to say?" she asked.

I leaned back on my left leg, pushed forward with my right, dipped across the room, and stopped at the Sheila E. poster I had taped to my closet door. "You step up to her in your clean lavender, lime-green, or sunshine-yellow suit and matching gators. A pimp always gotta be sharp. Then you wink your eye and say, 'Ah 'scuse me, but you fine as wine. Soft like butter. Pretty as a Georgia peach. What's a beauty like you doin' out in these mean streets? You need me to take you home? You can't stay out here 'cause the wolf will eat up somethin' this sweet. Are you hungry? Let me buy you something to eat.' You never let her answer. You just slide her a couple dollars."

"A couple dollars? Word?"

"Word. That's called an investment."

Yvette shook her head and her box braids swung over her shoulders. "I ain't givin' no money away. Not me. 'Specially not to no ho."

"She ain't your ho yet. And anyway, once you slide her some dough, she gon' immediately drop her head down and smile, like they all do. That's when you lift her chin." I cupped Yvette's face in my right hand. "You ask her name, and no matter what she tells you, you change it."

Yvette slapped my hand from her face. "Change it? Why?"

"You gotta break her in. Make her be what you want her to be. And you start by changin' her name." I flopped back down on the bed, grabbed the *Right On!* magazine from my nightstand, and in between looking over at Yvette, I leafed through the pages and blew kisses at Kurtis Blow's picture.

"How you know what name to come up with though?" she asked.

"If you a righteous pimp, like my daddy, then whatever name you give her gon' stick and she gon' like it. You think Queenie's name is Queenie?"

Yvette gasped. "It ain't?"

"Heck no." I carefully ripped out a LL Cool J poster from the center of my magazine. "Queenie's name is Beverly. My daddy said when he saw her pretty red skin, deep dimples, and those soft freckles sprinkled across her cheeks, he knew she was gon' be queen of these streets. And she is. Well, she used to be. Now she stay home and sling rock. She always trippin' though. Don't know how to be quiet, she stay outta pocket and Daddy stay gettin' her together. But nothin' he does will get Queenie to listen."

"Why won't she listen?"

"I don't know." I hunched my shoulders, got off the bed, and taped my new poster over my nightstand. Then I leaned back and smiled at it.

"Maybe she tired of your daddy beatin' on her."

Wait…what? I whipped around toward Yvette. *Oh no, she didn't!* "See. You 'bout to blow my high and that's why you ain't gon' be no pimp. How you gon' say somethin' like that? Any pimp worth his salt in the game ain't gon' let no new ho, old ho, or ex ho shine on him. And anyway, since you all in my daddy's bizness, know this: My daddy is a family man. Er'body knows Queenie is special to him and once she learns to listen, he'll stop pulling his belt off. Now don't talk about my daddy no more."

"I wasn't talkin' about your daddy. Mph, at least you got one. All I got is Nana and she makes me babysit while she chase the Holy Ghost er'night."

I shook my head, feeling sorry for Yvette. She really didn't have anybody. Her mother had three babies with my uncle Ray, my daddy's brother. Uncle Ray and Yvette's mother left Yvette and the kids they had together with Nana. So I guess you could say Yvette was family, but not really family. "Who's your real father, Yvette?"

She smacked her lips and opened the last pack of Pop Rocks. "A question mark and the only person with the answer is my mother. And you know she on a drug run."

"That's messed up. Yo' mama need to take a chill pill. She just jetted and Nana done practically made you a slave. Always babysittin'." I sat in my wicker throne chair. "They not yo' kids. Yo' mama needs to come off her drug run and handle her scandal."

"I know."

"Matter fact. You need to run away. Come live with me. We don't go to church and ain't no lil kids to babysit."

Her face lit up. "Word?"

"Word. Besides, Queenie ain't gon' care."

"Yo' daddy?"

"He won't even notice."

"Okay. I have to ask Nana first, though."

"Ask her? What kind of runaway asks to leave?"

Yvette's eyes grew wide. "I have to ask."

Whatever. That runaway plan was the dumbest I'd ever heard. "Well, let me know how that works out for you."

"I will…" Yvette said, getting up from the bed and walking over to the window. She pressed her face into the pane and the end of her nose smudged the glass. She pointed out into the courtyard. "I wanna tell you a secret, but you gotta promise not to tell anybody."

"Who I'ma tell? You already know I don't have a big mouth."

"I know."

"So tell me."

"You know who I think is cute?"

"Face?"

"That's not a secret."

"Well then, who?"

She stared at me, her eyes sizing me up. "You better not tell nobody."

"Who is it?"

"Cross your heart and hope to die."

"Just tell me!"

"Cross your heart."

"Okay, okay, cross my heart. I'm not gon' hope to die though. It's too many suckers gettin' killed around here so I ain't jinxin' myself. Now tell me."

"Flip." A smile bloomed across her face. "And he told me that he liked me too but—"

I almost spat on my floor in disgust. I dry heaved and air hurled. "Yoooooo, that's gotta be the nastiest mess that I've ever heard in my life. Ill! He is old as dirt!"

"No, he's not. He's only twenty-eight years old and—"

"That's like Jesus old. He older than Moses. And he nasty. He be out there looking at all the young girls' butts, tryna get wit' er'body. Don't fall for that. He's a cavity creep. Yuck muck."

"Would you calm down? I just said I thought he was cute. I didn't say I liked him back."

"I hope not. Plus, I heard he on dust."

"Psst, please. He is not on no dust and anyway, I don't wanna talk about it no more."

"So what you wanna do?"

"I want you to come on so I can go to the store and steal me some more jelly bracelets."

4

License to ill

"'Ey, yo, where you been?" Face's grill was blurred behind a cloud of weed smoke as he brazenly sat on the edge of *my* bed and knocked off the last of *my* roach. The *same roach* me and Yvette had plans to come back in here and finish. And yeah, Face was my favorite brother, but still, I was two seconds from puttin' my size sixes in his chest.

"You must be tryna get cussed out." I looked him over from his high-top fade to the cinnamon freckles speckled across his face. "Yo' red behind smoked the last of my weed. Is you crazy?" I shook my head. "You know what? The next time you bust up in here it's gon' be a problem for you."

He smiled and his front gold tooth gleamed. I looked over at Yvette and her face was lit up like a Christmas tree.

Face winked at Yvette and said, "I came to check on you two. Make sure you was all good."

A smile bloomed across my face. *"Shiiiiiiiiiiiit."* I

walked over to Face, slapped him five on the black hand side, and then flicked my nose in pride. "I'm surprised Queenie didn't wait for you to come back before she left. So she could brag about how my work was decent. Yvette put a lock in Aiesha's head and I left the white meat of her cheek flappin'."

"Word." Yvette grinned, sitting down next to Face as I sat down in my throne chair. She carried on, "We let that herb know we ain't the ones. Betchu won't none of 'em come for us again."

"I betchu they won't either," Face said, walkin' over to the boom box and admirin' it. "This is ill. Where you get it from?"

"We jacked it." Yvette twirled one of her braids.

Face smiled. "From who?"

"Who you think?" Yvette said sweetly. "Aiesha. The broad we left bleeding in the street."

"That's wassup." He balanced the equalizer.

"Faaaaaaace," Yvette whined. "We got some candy. You want some?" She held up the pack of Pop Rocks and candy cigarettes we'd just stolen. I sucked my teeth. Truthfully, I couldn't understand what Yvette saw in Face. All I knew was that whenever he came around, she'd turned into a real ding-a-ling dumb and love-struck clown. Straight stupid. No respect for us being play cousins. And she didn't seem to notice that all Face offered her was a smile. She still pushed up on him.

I yanked the candy outta her hands and rolled my eyes. "Psych." I sat back down. "Yvette, you better stop playin'. You wanna give him somethin'? Give him them jelly bracelets, them earrings, or that name ring you got on." I turned back to Face. "And anyway, I got a bone to pick witchu."

"Wassup?" He turned away from the boom box and leaned against the window sill.

" 'Ey, why of all the D-boys you can have slangin' for you, you got some Down South fools out there?"

Face looked at me like I was crazy. "What? Down South? Whatchu talkin' 'bout? You already know I don't get down like that."

"Well, then you got a problem. 'Cause when me and Yvette was walking back from the store, the one on the corner of Jeliff and Muhammad Ali, in front of the town houses, was straight boomin'. Them boys was servin' all kinda fools."

Face frowned and his whole face wrinkled. "You sure? They was out there slangin'?"

I smirked at him and arched a brow.

"The corner of Jeliff? In front of the town houses?"

"Yup."

"How many was out there clockin'?"

I looked over at Yvette. "It was about five, six?"

Yvette nodded her head. "Yeah, about six."

"How you know they was from Down South?"

" 'Cause one of 'em tried to kick it to me," I said. "He served a fiend, then looked up and was like, ''Ey, yo, you lookin' ripe, shawty, how old is you? Fifteen?' "

The veins in Face's neck thumped, but he never raised his voice. That's how I knew he was madder than hell. "And what you say?" he asked.

I smiled and said, " 'Yeah. I'm fifteen.' Then me and Yvette kept on walkin'."

Face nodded. His hazel eyes danced with pissed-off thoughts. "A'ight. A'ight. A'ight. Good lookin' out. I'ma head out. I need to see wassup."

I did my best to push away my giggles and I knew Yvette was doing the same thing. But once Face broke out the room, I walked over to Yvette and both of us fell across my bed and cracked up. "Yooooooo," Yvette said. "He was mad!"

"Hell yeah. You can't set up shop on somebody's block. Nah. Fools get killed for less than that. And you know Face gon' handle 'em."

"I wish I could watch."

"Me too." I grinned. "I know one thing though. I can't wait to get to school on Monday."

"Me either."

"'Cause er'body gon' be talking about two things: us bum-rushin' Aiesha and Ninety-five South goin' home in garbage bags."

5

It's like a jungle sometimes

Ten p.m.

The moment Daddy did a drunk strut past my room with the lingering scent of lavender and stale Thunderbird trailing behind him, I knew the spot was 'bout to blow up. So I sprang to my feet and followed him.

Daddy rushed into he and Queenie's bedroom and slammed the door behind him. I squatted, leaned into the peephole, and watched the action unfold.

Queenie lay back on their bed, with a coffee-colored knee-high on her head. She was dressed in a beige half a slip and a black lace bra, and she held a thin brown cigarette in the corner of her lips as she watched TV.

"Where you go this afternoon, Queenie? Huh?!" Daddy walked over to the TV and turned it off. "Answer me! You didn't ask me if you could go anywhere!" Daddy unbuckled his brown leather belt and snatched it off.

Queenie eased the cigarette from between her lips and blew a cloud of smoke toward him. "Last I checked, I was grown. Now what you *can* do is wash off that stankin' perfume and sleep off that Thunderbird. Or you can carry yo' raggedy ass back to building 272 and play daddy to the two lil baldheaded bastards you think nobody knows about. Now I'm warnin' you. 'Cause tonight"—she shook her index finger at him—"is not yo' night."

"You think you better than me?! Huh? You think you can just do what you wanna do around here?" Daddy moved in closer to her.

"You better get yo' drunk behind somewhere and sit down!" Queenie grabbed onto the edge of the bed, where she kept the knife tucked under the mattress, but before she could reach it, Daddy reared the belt back, and sent her tumbling to the floor. "You don't ever tell me what to do!" He took a step back and stumbled into the dresser.

Queenie picked herself up. The hem of her slip was torn and hanging and her bra straps draped off her shoulders. She licked the bloody corner of her swollen bottom lip, carefully slid a blade from between her teeth, and sailed it down the side of Daddy's face.

My heart stopped.

I couldn't breathe.

"Whatchu doin'?" Schooly said from behind my back, scarin' me. "Pops and Queenie already told you about bustin' into they room. You gon' get in trouble."

I spun around. "She just sliced his face! Don't you hear them in there fightin'! You wasn't sleepin' that hard."

Schooly shrugged. "So? And? What I care if he got his face sliced. Maybe he deserved it."

I wanted to steal on Schooly and lay a fist right in his jaw for sayin' somethin' stupid like that. "You sound so dumb!"

"I'm not dumb! I'm smart. I'm smart enough to know that when I turn eighteen, I'ma get a good job, and then me and Queenie will be outta here!"

"Why we gotta wait that long? You *and Queenie* can roll right now—"

"What the hell y'all doin'?!" Queenie snatched the door open and her left eye looked like purple and black rolls of neck fat. The nastiness made me squint.

Schooly took off. But I didn't. I slid to the left of Queenie and peeked back into she and Daddy's bedroom. Daddy was bent over at the waist and holding a blood-soaked towel up to his face.

"Daddy!" I said in a panic. "You okay?"

Before he could answer, Queenie stepped completely into the hallway and pulled the door shut. "Take your behind back to the bed!" she said and then swished toward the bathroom.

I followed her. Leaned against the door frame and watched her look at herself in the medicine cabinet's mirror. She inspected the flamin'-red belt-buckle marks beat into her right cheek. Then she lifted her gaze and stared at my reflection. I knew then we was thinking the same thing: she was crazy.

Queenie reached in the medicine cabinet and pulled out a bottle of peroxide. She shuffled a few bottles of Tylenol around before sucking her teeth and pushing past me. "Schooly!" She walked to my brothers' room and peeked over Face's empty bed at Schooly's. She frowned and shook her head. "Schooly!"

This sucker was stretched out and snoring, like he wasn't just talkin' smack to me, less than five minutes ago.

"Boy, you ain't asleep. Get up. I need you to go to the

store for me!" Queenie grabbed the end of his sheet and yanked it.

Schooly yawned, stretched, and slowly peeled his eyes open. Both me and Queenie rolled our eyes to the ceiling. The only difference was Queenie lowered her gaze and smiled at Schooly while I ice grilled him.

"Listen, baby," Queenie said in a soft tone. "Mama needs you to go to the store for her and get some gauze and tape so I can patch up your daddy." She turned to me. "Isis, go get my purse off the kitchen table."

I did as she said and quickly returned. She handed Schooly five dollars. "And get me an ice-cold Pepsi. 'Cause my nerves is shot."

Schooly didn't move; instead, he lay there, obviously soaking in every one of Queenie's bruises.

Queenie turned away. "Boy, what did I tell you to do!" she said, walking out his bedroom door.

He hopped up in a huff. Tryna play it off like he was mad about being sent to the store, when I could clearly see that he was mad about how Queenie looked.

"And come right back! And don't get in no trouble," Queenie yelled behind him as he stormed out the front door.

"Can I ask you somethin'?" I said, as Queenie walked toward her bedroom.

She spun around, her eyes was loaded with a million thoughts. "What?"

"Ain't you tired of Daddy beatin' on you? 'Cause I know I am."

Silence.

I continued, "You know what I think?" I tapped my foot, anxious for her to say yes.

She didn't answer. But I could tell by the way she lifted her good eye that she wanted to know, so I continued on. "I think if you stopped doin' things without askin' him and learned to be quiet sometimes, Daddy won't have to get mad and you won't have to cut 'im."

Queenie stared at me so long and hard that I knew she was about to beat me down. I took a step back. Prepared to take off runnin' and never stop.

Instead of her gunnin' for my life or snatchin' me by the throat, she placed a hand up on her hip and said, "How about if you shut your mouth. Stay out of me and my man's affairs, and stay in a child's place. Now getcho fresh behind outta my face before you find yourself wakin' up dead and buried in the middle of next week!"

6

Ain't no half steppin'

The next afternoon

"**Y**ou better getcho behind outta my face before you wake up dead and buried in the middle of next week!"

"*Yooooooo*, she said that?" Yvette's eyes bugged and danced in delight, as if she admired the way Queenie had played me.

"Yup. Ain't she trippin'?" I tossed into the air, just to see if Yvette would agree or not, 'cause if she was my best friend and for-real play cousin, then she would be on my side. But if she wasn't...I was gon' gut her like a fish.

Her face wrinkled. "Heck yeah, she trippin'. Hard."

I smiled and bopped my head to the music. Somebody's black Maxima, which was parked half on the street and half on the sidewalk, pumped Tenor Saw's "Pumpkin Belly."

Me and Yvette was sittin' in the middle of the courtyard, on the top of a concrete park bench, and across from Face and his boy Ke'Ron.

Ke'Ron, who the streets called K-Rock. 'Cause he boxed and when he threw a jab his opponents always said it felt like he had a bolder in his hands.

K-Rock who I secretly loved.

And dreamed loved me back.

And wanted to marry me.

And have pretty babies with me.

Who I thought looked just like the caramel version of Michael Jackson, the one on the *Thriller* album. Minus the Jheri curl and the Tinkerbell voice.

K-Rock was the color of apple butter. Scratch that. He was the color of the *sweetest* apple butter. His almond-shaped eyes was a sparkling marble brown. His hair was a low Caesar with a thousand spinning waves, and his gear was fresh to def. Er'day. All day.

I think he was seventeen.

But I wasn't exactly sure.

He slang with Face on the weekends, but during the week K-Rock went to school, something we all found out last year that Face didn't do. Queenie cried and slapped him when she realized he'd dropped out. But who could blame Face? It's not like he was stupid, but he was seventeen in the ninth grade. So he left and never went back. Shortly after that, Queenie and Daddy said he was a man.

And now he ran things. I just wished he would run his friend over here to me.

I looked over at Yvette and she was staring at Face just as hard as I'd been staring at K-Rock. A few seconds later, Yvette looked at me and we both bust out laughin', knowin' that in our thoughts we was brides-to-be, which is why I said, "We should have a double wedding."

Yvette's face lit up. "Word. That would be the bomb. And you know who we could have sing at our wedding?"

"Who?"

"New Edition."

"Ohhhhhh my Goooooood! Yes! And we could have my daddy walk us both down the aisle."

"I would love that. And just so you know, I'm not wearing white. I'ma wear pink 'cause that's my favorite color."

"Eww, you gon' look like a skeezer too. You gotta wear white 'cause that's what brides do."

"Bride?" came from behind us. "Who gettin' married?" That was my girl Grier, who we called Munch 'cause she stayed having the munchies. And she didn't even smoke weed that much. She just liked to eat.

"What up, Munch?!" me and Yvette said simultaneously, looking over at the girl standing next her, immediately sizing her up. She was short. About five feet even, thin, with a bra full of boobs, and white. Like for-real white. Not extremely high yellow. Not albino. Not mulatto. Not Mexican. White. Pale peach-colored skin. Icy gray eyes. Dark brown silky hair that she pulled back in a ponytail. She wasn't a white fiend that roamed or hoed around here. And she looked too young to be five-oh. So clearly she was in the wrong hood.

"Who dis?" Yvette asked, curling her top lip.

"Took the question outta my mouth." I popped my lips.

The white girl wiggled her neck. "My name is Catherine."

Me and Yvette's mouths dropped open. Catherine looked straight up like Brooke Shields but, sounded as if her name should've been Shonda. Or Lisa. Or Myeesha.

"This is my foster sister," Munch said, shoving a hand full of Crunchy Cheez Doodles in her mouth. "Told you my cousin Shake and his wife was foster parents. Catherine came to live with us yesterday. She cool."

"A'ight." I smiled and said, "If you cool with Munch, then good with us."

"Yup," Yvette agreed.

"So, Catherine, you can chill wit' us when we go to school on Monday," I said. "We call our crew the Get Fresh Clique. The all-girl version of the Get Fresh Crew. And just so you know Doug E. Fresh is my husband."

"You like Doug E. Fresh?" She smiled. "That's my man. Step off."

I tried to not laugh but failed, and a small giggle slipped out. "Whatever. You better go check for one of the Beastie Boys, 'cause I had Doug E. first."

Catherine did her all to look tough but couldn't hold it up. "You can have him." She grinned and snapped her fingers. "I been diggin' this lil dude named Too $hort anyway. He's from Cali and he is everything and more."

I laughed. "You been to Cali?"

"Yeah. I used to live there with my father."

"What part?" My eyes opened wide. I was hoping she was going to say Hollywood.

"Oakland."

I felt deflated. "Word?"

"Yup."

I hesitated; then, as if a light bulb had gone off, I said, "I got it. We gon' call you Cali. 'Cause that's cute and that's where you from. Catherine sounds like a nun or somebody's great-grandmama. Let the teachers call you Catherine, but your peoplez gon' call you Cali."

Cali stood quiet for a moment, chewing the corner of her thin bottom lip. "Cali...Cali...ummm, I like that."

"That's stupid fresh, yo," Munch said.

Cali's eyes beamed in pride. "Yeah. That is dope."

I continued, "Now, Cali, how you get to Brick City?"

"My dad died. And my mother lived in Bloomfield, New Jersey, with her boyfriend. So I had to live with them."

"Why you don't live with them now?" Yvette asked.

Cali whispered, "She put me out."

"How old are you?" I had to ask.

"Thirteen."

"And she put you out?" I asked in disbelief. "What, you slept with her man or somethin'?"

"No." Cali shook her head. "He slept with me."

We all fell silent, knowing exactly what that meant. I wanted to ask more questions. But we'd just met this chick and I didn't need her buggin' out 'cause I was all in her business.

"Yooooooo," Munch said, breaking up the awkward silence. "Ain't that Flip?" She pointed.

I curled my top lip. "Yeah, with his nasty butt. Always tryna talk to girls our age knowing he twenty-eight."

"He a fiend?" Munch asked.

"Yup," I added, watching Flip and Face give each other a loaded fist bump. "He be over there coppin' all the time."

"You don' know if he coppin' or not," Yvette snapped. "He might just be saying hi to Face."

"And what you taking up for Flip for?" I asked. "I knooooow you not checkin' for him."

"No. I'm not. I'm just saying y'all need to stop doggin' him."

Me and Munch jerked our necks back and looked at Yvette like she stank; then we each flicked our wrists and waved our hands. "He's a fiend," we said simultaneously.

"Whatever," Yvette snapped. "Let's get back to planning our double wedding."

"I'm marrying Ralph Tresvant." Cali snapped her fingers. "Yes! What! Don't play me."

We all fell out laughing, and just as I was about to confess my love for Ke'Ron Green, Face stepped over to us, winked his eye at my friends, then looked at me. "I need to holler at you for a minute, lil sis."

I frowned. "Can't you wait until I get home later? You see I'm kickin' it with my friends. You see this."

Face chuckled, but not a funny chuckle, an edgy one that let me know he was serious. "I *said* I need to holler atchu real quick."

I sucked my teeth as I raised up off the park bench and jumped to the ground. I looked back at my girls and said, "Give me a minute."

Me and Face walked for two blocks before I finally said, "Ummm...helloooooo...I know you didn't stop me and my friends from kickin' it to come and take a stroll with you. You could've called one of your skeezers for this."

Face frowned as we made a left turn into Eighteenth Avenue School's playground. We hopped up on the short brick wall and sat down. "What's up with you?" I pressed. "'Cause I don't have much time. I got a wedding to plan."

"A weddin'?" He flicked his wrist, like what I said was ridiculous. "Look, ever since you told me about them dudes trying to move in on me I've been trying to decide if you were a big enough girl to chill with me or not. Move up to the major leagues."

I looked up at him out the corner of my eyes. "Major leagues?"

"Yeah, major leagues."

"And what you want me do? Cuss out another chick for you? What? Go to her house this time? Face, did you beat up another broad? Didn't Queenie tell you about your hands?"

"See, it ain't even nothin' like that."

"Then what is it? Don't tell me somebody else is pregnant? Why is you exploding in everybody? You nasty. And Queenie and Daddy both told you to use condoms."

"Yo, would you chill?"

"I'm chilled." I paused. "What, you want me to hold your stash for you?"

"Are you gon' let me talk?"

"I wish you would, 'cause I'm tired of sitting here wondering what you want. Talk."

"I want you to come ride out with me and assist me on this drop."

A drop? My eyes scanned his face. He was serious. I did all I could to not grin. But I couldn't help it. My smile was lit from ear to ear. No matter how many times I begged him, Face never let me ride out with him before. The most he would let me do was handle his irrelevant chicks by cussing them out. Or take me out to the vacant lot and teach me how to squeeze off a round or two. But that was it. No drops. No licks. And no hits. Until now.

I wanted to scream out, "Yes!" Then jump up and moonwalk across the brick ledge. But I didn't. I played it cool. After all he was checkin' for me. I didn't come looking for him. "I don't know if I need to do that," I said, leaning back, reaching in my side jeans pocket and taking out a candy cigarette.

"What?" He frowned and then laughed. "Stop playin', son."

"Word to the mother, I'm not playing." I took a chalky pull and blew a puff of powdery smoke into the air. "All the times I asked you to let me ride and you played me for your boy K-Rock."

"K-Rock is my homie."

"Well, then ride out with him. I'm good." I crossed my legs and stuffed the rest of the cigarette into my mouth, turning the chalky stick into stiff gum.

"He's already on the drop. And he agreed that you should ride out with us. You would be our element of surprise."

My eyes grew wide and my heart thundered in my chest. *K-Rock did what?* I almost drooled. "Oh really." I mustered up a fake frown.

"Yeah. Plus you ready. You handled your business the other day without hesitation so I think you can handle this."

"You think so?" I nodded. "A'ight, so what you want me to do?"

7

You be illin'

At 11:47 PM, Face looked at me for the third time and said, "You sure you ready? 'Cause, word is bond, you cannot be freezin' up. You said you wanted to be a big girl so I need you to be about this big money."

Me and Face was in the cut, parked in a small alleyway. We sat in his black Monte Carlo, with the lights off, and I promise you I wanted to take my fist and throat bust 'im. Make 'im cough his tonsils up. And yeah, I was scared as heck. It was one thing to imagine what a drop would be like, but it was a whole other level to be about it in real life.

However.

I didn't need Face sweating me like this. I needed him to hype me up. Make me feel like I was that chick. Instead, he made my stomach queasy, like I had diarrhea.

Sweat bubbled on my nose and brow. I wiped it with the back of my hand, then turned and looked straight at Face. "First of all, I don't like how you comin' at me, all wild and crazy, like you doubtin' me. And second of all, if you didn't trust me then you should've left me at home. 'Cause me and Yvette got a bag of weed to smoke. And I got school tomorrow. Now either you wanna do this or you don't. 'Cause you gotcha boy up the street."

I pointed through the windshield at K-Rock, who'd just stepped outta his car and was kickin' it with one of the Down South dudes who'd moved in on Face's block. "And he's all ready for the kill. But you sittin' here and sweatin' me like you on your period. You need a maxi pad or some-thin'?"

"I don't know who you think you talking to, but I ain't Schooly. So you better watch yo' mouth and chill wit' all that. I'm just making sure you know that once we get outta this car, that this not a game."

I swallowed the nerves I felt tingling my throat and twisted my lips. "Yo, look, is you ready?"

"I'm ready."

I tossed Face his ski mask and slid mine over my face and neck. "Well, let's go get 'em."

We eased out the car and tipped a few steps down the block. I was doing my best not to give in to the nerves dancing around in my stomach. I squeezed my inner thighs tightly, as we walked up behind 'em. There were three dudes, including K-Rock, chopping it up and han-dling business. K-Rock was to pretend that he was buying the pounds of weed and that he was just as surprised as the other dudes when we snuck up behind them.

Click-click! Pop-pop!

Face bust two shots in the air and er'body froze.

"ER'BODY HIT THE GROUND! FACE DOWN!" Face yelled and they all hit the concrete.

"Ice," Face spat quickly. "Run the car real quick. Check the glove compartment. Under the seats, the sides of the doors, and the trunk. Take everything you see!"

The car was a silver Audi 5000, kitted up. Truthfully, we should've just taken the car, stripped it, and taken it to the chop shop, but obviously Face didn't think of that. And there was no time to toss a monkey wrench in the plan, so I did as I was told. In the glove compartment was a nine and a thirty-eight. Under the seats was pounds of weed and two more guns. And in the trunk was two pots of gold at the end of the rainbow: one duffel bag full of money, mostly hundred-dollar bills. And another duffel bag filled with raw dope.

Cha-ching!

When I hopped out the car, I saw one of the dudes on the ground inching his hand around toward his boot. I rushed over to him, kicked away his hand, then kicked him in his side. "Word is bond, you 'bout to have two choices: this three-fifty-seven to the dome or this forty-five in your throat!"

Click-click! Face readied the gun.

I carried on, "Now try some sucker shit again and see don't yo' mama be dressed in all black." I snatched a twenty-two from the side of his shoe.

I looked up at Face and could tell by the way his eyes shined that beneath his ski mask he was grinnin'. "Hurry up. Run they pockets!" he spat.

I hit up all of their pockets, including K-Rock, 'cause I had to make it seem like he wasn't a part of the plan.

I snatched wads of money, baggies filled with vials of crack, and two more guns. Afterwards, I made them take off every stitch of jewelry they had on: gold watches, gold chains, and rings. "And spit out them grills too!" I said and out came two diamond-clustered grills on the ground. I tossed everything into the duffel bag.

A few seconds later, we were back in the car. We tossed the ski masks into the street, and sped off into the distance.

I swear I'd never felt no high like this before. I felt like I was...on top of the world. Walking on clouds. Like I was in Oz. I couldn't believe I'd just pulled that off. Truth be told, I wanted to go again. My heart thundered in my chest and although I wanted to ask Face how he thought I was, I couldn't stop smiling long enough to speak.

When we got back to Da Bricks, K-Rock was waiting for us in our building. We didn't make no eye contact with him; instead, we were silent, and walked quietly to our apartment.

Marvin Gaye's "Sexual Healing" serenaded us as we walked into the living room. Daddy was holding Queenie's hand and leading her to their bedroom, leaving the turntable spinning.

Me and K-Rock followed Face into he and Schooly's room. Schooly was sleeping or at least pretending that he was.

Face flicked the light on, and just as he started grinning at me, K-Rock gave me a hug so tight that I didn't ever want him to let me go.

God, he smelled delicious.

I wrapped my arms around him and sank my head into his hard chest.

I wonder if he have a six- or an eight-pack.

"Yooooooooo, Icy, you be illin'!" K-Rock smiled.

Icy? Did he just call me Icy? That is soooooo hot....I think I wanna change my name.

"Word is bond, you the illest lil sis in the world."

Illest lil sis...? I dropped my arms, held my head up, and stepped out of his embrace.

"Word up," Face said. "You did that. I was so proud of you, I ain't know what to do. I got another drop I'ma need you to hit up with me! Straight up."

Face yanked one of the duffel bags from the floor, while K-Rock picked up the other.

I stood there, tapping my foot, as K-Rock and Face divvied up the goods. I was getting pissed by the moment, but instead of spazzing out I simply said, "Y'all tryna play me or somethin'?"

They both turned and looked at me. Even Schooly quickly opened his eyes and then closed them back.

Face and K-Rock looked surprised. "Nah, Icy," K-Rock said. "Wassup?"

"First of all *Ke'Ron*, my name is not Icy. It's Isis. And what you mean, wassup? Wassup?" I frowned. "You know what time it is!" I held my hand out.

"Oh my bad," Face said. "Let me hit you off real quick." He handed me a fifty-dollar bill, a gold chain, and a ring.

Oh. Hell. No. He didn't.

And just when I didn't think it could get worse, K-Rock handed me a gold watch and said, "I thought about keeping this for myself, but here you go, Icy."

I slid the money in my pocket, but everything else I tossed alongside of Schooly. "I know you not asleep, Schooly. And you can have all that." Schooly opened his eyes long enough to sweep his new jewelry collection under his pillow and then he turned toward the wall and closed his eyes again.

I lifted a nine and thirty-eight from the dresser. I didn't

know if the guns had bullets in them or not, but I still pointed 'em anyway. "The way I see it, just like I told them soft mothersuckers tonight. You got two choices. This nine or this thirty-eight 'cause one thing y'all not about to do is play me out. I was an equal part of the drop and I want some of that money. Now y'all fools can have the dope and the weed, but that money, I need at least twenty bills outta there. Period."

Face frowned. "Yo, you buggin'. Put them guns down."

K-Rock smiled at me and I hated that all I could think about was how beautiful his teeth were.

"I ain't puttin' nothin' down, until you put my money up. You got at least a hundred grand in that bag. Now don't let me get Queenie in here 'cause you already know she'll keep all the dope, the weed, and take half ya money just on G.P. Now try me. I said twenty bills, but since you have pissed me off even more. I need twenty-one."

They laughed.

"You think this is funny?" I knocked the safety off the guns. "And you think I'ma put back on my ski mask? And this is how you handle your business? Oh, you dead wrong. And K-Rock, don't let Face supe you up. 'Cause Face already know how I gets down."

"You trippin'." Face shook his head.

"No, you trippin'. Now cough it up."

I watched them count out twenty one-hundred-dollar bills. "Now hand them to Schooly."

Schooly turned over and sat up. Face handed him the money.

I put the safety back on the guns and set them on the dresser. I took all but three bills from Schooly. "You can have that."

Then I turned back to Face and K-Rock. "Nice doing business with you." I pointed to the rest of the goods. "Now back to your regularly scheduled program. Nah mean." I hit 'em off with a smile. Walked back to my room, tossed the money on the bed, and giggled as I stretched my arms out and landed on it.

8

Sucker MCs

"**I**SIS, THE POLICE HERE!"

"Whatchu talkin' 'bout, Willis?" poured from the TV as Schooly flung my room door open, freakin' out. Tears a blink away from fallin' from his eyes.

I was in the middle of getting dressed for school when my heart fell through the floor.

I pulled Schooly into my room and pushed the door closed. Drew in a breath. And held it. Until it kicked its way outta my mouth.

The cops.

I wanted to die. Right now. Right here. I couldn't believe it.

"Where is Daddy and Queenie?"

He hunched his shoulders. "They ain't here. And I'm scared. What you and Face do last night?" Schooly's eyes wildly combed me from head to toe.

Sweat bubbled across my brow, my nose, and my palms felt clammy. I whispered, "We did a lick, that's it. Some dudes was tryna move in on Face's turf. And we handled 'em."

"They still breathin'?"

"Yeah, they breathin'. Unless somebody else sent the grim reaper. But we didn't."

"You sure?"

I hesitated. "Wait. What? I know you don't think they here for me?! Do you?!"

Schooly shook his head. "No. I don't think they here just for you. I think they here for you *and* Face."

"Don't be sayin' that!"

"Well, that's what I think."

My stomach was balled into a knot that grew tighter by the moment. "Face here?"

"Yep. He's in our room asleep."

"We gotta wake him up!"

I placed my hand on the knob, but before I could twist it, "POLICE OPEN UP!" blared from the other side.

"Schooly." My eyes bugged and my breathing was heavy. "Why they sound so close? Did they knock the door down?!"

"No! Not this time. Last time I got hit upside the head when the door flew off the hinges. I wasn't gon' let that happen again, so I opened the door for 'em. They standing in the living room."

"The living room?!" My stomach bubbled and dropped to my feet. "You let them in this house and yo' behind just had me confess?! What, you workin' wit' five-oh? They gotchu wired or somethin'?!" I mushed him on the side of his head and an ever-ready stream of pee split in two and zipped down both of my legs. I squeezed my inner thighs to hold back what I could. But, I knew at any moment that Schooly and I would both be standing in a puddle of piss.

I placed my palms on the sides of my temples and squeezed.

Think...think...think...

When I couldn't get a thought through I looked around my room from the faded white walls covered with smeared fingerprints and hip-hop posters, to my twin-sized bed, my wicker throne chair, the single dresser wit' the lopsided drawers and the clothes bursting from the top.

There was nowhere to hide in here.

The closet.

No. Queenie said don't ever hide in the closet. Pigs always look for you there.

The window.

We're on the third floor. I could jump.

I ran over to the window. There was no way I could get through the black iron security bars and even if I could, the cops had the courtyard blocked and their blaring blue lights lit up the morning sky.

"I can't go to jail!" Tears filled my eyes and I felt like taking my fist and pounding Schooly in his slow head with it. I promise you, even though he went to a special school, I never believed he was all-the-way retarded, until now. "Ugggggggggg! What the heck is wrong with you?! You not stupid. You a lil slow, but you not stupid. You don't open no door for no freakin' cops. Whyyyyyyyy would you do that?!"

"OPEN UP! AND COME OUT WITCHA HANDS UP!" The police hammered against my bedroom door and I knew from the last time they rammed the front door down and dragged Daddy out, that it was only a matter of seconds before they'd be doing the same thing to me.

Before I could decide what to do, "FREEZE! GET ON THE FLOOR AND PUT YOUR ARMS WHERE WE CAN SEE 'EM!" filled the room and the familiar sounds of shufflin' police boots muddied the air. Me and Schooly both hit the deck. I held both of my arms out. And Schooly did his best.

One of the officers walked over and stared down at us. "Get up! And turn around. Slowly."

We did. And faced a room full of at least ten cops in dark blue uniforms and guns drawn. "Put your guns away," the lead officer demanded.

They retreated and I wondered if they was about to handcuff me. Instead, the lead officer gripped me by the forearm and dragged me into the living room. Another cop dragged Schooly out behind me.

The cop who gripped me up curled his upper lip in disgust and spat, "Little girl, where is the derelict and the pimp at?" And he said that like derelicts and pimps was a problem for him.

I didn't answer, 'cause I didn't have to. I swear I could practically hear Schooly's thoughts, and when I heard him pull in a gulp of air, I whipped my head toward him and said, tight-lipped, "You bet not say nothin'."

"And why not? What shouldn't he say?!" The cop pushed his chest into my face, the metal buttons in the center of his uniform shirt kissed my nose.

I took a step back and bumped into the wall behind me. *Breathe. Breathe. You got this.*

I looked up at the cop and slammed my hands up on my hips. "Whatchu want wit' my daddy and my brother?"

"Where are they? Are they out there in the street turning little girls into prostitutes?"

He trippin'. And he got me and my family *alllllll* the way twisted. Ain't no way I'ma let this pig talk about the Carters like that. Cop. Or no cop. I looked up and into this fool's peach-colored face and said, "No. They out turnin' yo' blue-eyed mama into one."

Now how you like that!

I could tell I'd caught him off guard by the way he lifted his left hand, reared it back, and froze midway in the slap he'd obviously intended to lay across my face.

I flinched. Just a little. But then I did my best to regain my stance and boldly looked back into his face. "What you buggin' for?! They ain't here. Ain't nobody here but us! So you and yo' squad can leave! You don't have no right bustin' up in here. You don't have no warrant!"

"So then why am I here?" He paused. Sneered. Looked me over. "Huh? Answer me."

I didn't.

He continued, "You know that your father and your brother is the reason I'm here, don't you? You know that we have warrants for their arrests, don't you?"

"Warrants? Psst. Please." I shook my head in disgust. Pig stayed makin' things up.

The head pig continued, "You know that they been committing a string of strong-armed robberies don't you? Including the one they did last night, where they shot the gas attendant."

Last night? Now I know they lying. 'Cause me and Face was out on a lick and Daddy was probably laid up and drunk at the clean-up woman's house.

The cop continued, "Now where are the scumbags at?"

I shrugged and did my best to hold a blank stare. "I don't know what you talkin' 'bout."

"Oh, you know what I'm talking about."

"All I know is that don't nuffin' you just said gotta do wit' me or my brother, Schooly. So whatchu messin' wit us for?! And you know you foul for even being in here right now!"

"What the hell is goin' on up in here!" Queenie spat as she charged into the apartment. She briskly walked over to me and snatched me from the cop's face. I was now standing at her side. "Get over here, Schooly!" Schooly did as he was told and we were now all standing together. Queenie peered at the cops. "Why are you in my house?!"

"They said they lookin' for Daddy and Face!" I spat out.

"And why is that?" Queenie looked at the cop who was tryna chump me.

I continued, "Talkin' 'bout Daddy and Face did some strong-armed robberies." I twisted my lips. "Lies. Talkin' 'bout they shot some gas attendant last night. More lies. Straight bull. And to think they s'pose to protect and serve. Puhlease. And, Queenie, you already know Daddy was over there at Ms. Brenda's house last night with them two baldheaded lil babies he got, probably drunk. And me and Face was together. So they tellin' a bold-face lie. I swear to God, these blue fools stay trippin'!"

"Where is yo' warrant?" Queenie spat.

The lead cop swallowed and then said, "Ma'am, we just need to speak to them. Ask them a few questions."

"So you don't have no warrant!" Queenie shoved a hand up on her hip. "But my kids tryna get ready for school and you in here scaring 'em 'cause you wanna ask some questions. Get out!"

"Ma'am," the pig said. "We have a reason to believe that your son and husband may have some information about a string of gas station robberies and a shooting last night. They are persons of interest and we need to ask them some questions. Now where are they?"

"I don't know where they are!"

"Queenie." Schooly leaned into Queenie's ear, his voice trembling. "Face in the other room though."

Without batting an eye, Queenie said to the cop, "Unless

you got a warrant for they arrest, neither my husband nor my son will be talking to you or anybody else. Now get out!"

I swear I wanted to lay Schooly flat out with an uppercut. The cops ignored Queenie and walked to the back of the apartment, like they knew they way around here. They boldly flung Face's bedroom door open. All kinds of wrong.

"You cannot be coming up in here like this!" Queenie screamed. "You don't have no warrant and no right to be in here!" She blocked the doorway.

"Ma'am, if you don't move," the lead officer said, "I'm going to arrest you for interfering with an investigation."

Queenie still didn't move, but the cops pushed her slightly to the side and stepped into the room.

Face wasn't in the bed; he was hiding under it. "Come out," the lead pig said, "or we gon' come for you."

After a few seconds, Face slid from under the bed. The cops slapped cuffs on him and said, "We need you to come with us for questioning."

"Then what you cuffin' him for?!" I screamed, but the cops didn't answer me.

I couldn't believe this was happening and it was taking everything in me, or out of me, not to body-slam Schooly. Actually, I couldn't believe that Queenie hadn't beat me to it.

The lead cop smiled at Schooly on his way out and said, "Thank you, young man. You were a great help to us this morning."

Schooly grinned. "You're welcome. You know, I wanna be a cop when I grow up."

The cop winked, and as his counterparts walked Face out, he said, "Good luck with that." He paused and looked down at Schooly's arm. "Nice watch you got on, young man."

"Thank you, my sister gave it to me—"

"Shut. Up," Queenie said as she slammed the door behind the cops. And just when I thought she'd lost her touch and was a straight sucker, she backhanded Schooly so hard that his neck jerked back and I could swear that his head spun around and landed in yesterday.

9

Showstoppa

It seemed like the whole block was outside and waiting for me, just to be nosey and find out what happened with Face. Me and Queenie had already told Schooly that he better walk straight to that short yellow bus and keep his mouth shut. 'Cause what goes on in our house, stays in our house.

The moment I walked out of my building, I saw Yvette, Cali, and Munch sitting in the courtyard, on top of the park bench. "Isis. Wait up!" I heard Yvette say from behind me as I passed them.

"What's going on?" Cali asked, anxiously.

"Yeah, why the cops lock Face up this morning?" Munch asked, like she just had to know.

I sucked my teeth and I thought about flippin' all the way out. But I didn't. I waited for them to catch up to me, then I looked into their eager eyes and tripped. "Why y'all tricks all up in the Carter business? Did I butt into your family affairs, Munch, when the cops raided your apartment and locked your mama *and* grandmama up? Am I all in your situation, Yvette? And, Cali, you don't even know me like that." I looked her up and down. "So you need to step *allllllll* the way off."

The Get Fresh Clique looked at me and frowned. Then a few seconds later they fell out laughing.

Cali said, "Girl, please, if you don't stop trippin, homie."

"For real," Munch added.

"And we cousins, so you can tell me any and everything," Yvette insisted.

I wanted to take out my anger on them, but I could never stay mad at my girls for long. "It ain't no big deal really." I shrugged. "They holding him for questioning, and as long as he don't have no other warrants, he'll be home in two days. You know five-oh stay buggin'."

"Word." Cali shook her head.

"What they questioning him for?" Munch asked.

I sucked my teeth. "They talking about it's been a string of strong-arm robberies at some gas stations. And that a gas attendant was shot last night."

Yvette frowned and rolled her eyes. "They need to stop. That don't have nothing to do wit' Face. He ain't no thief like that. He only bring it to those in the game. That's it. He don't mess wit' civilians."

"Thank you!" My eyes bugged and I rocked my neck. "Exactly."

Munch carried on, "And anyway er'body know that it ain't one person doing those robberies. It's a buncha crackheads running up and down the block. And whoever got shot must've been playing hero, so they got popped. They should've just gave up the money and—"

"Hold up. Wait a minute." Cali laughed and pointed. "Who is that?"

"Where?" We all turned around and followed her short peach finger. She carried on, "It's a bird! It's a plane. It's Mr. T—"

"Oh, heck no! That's Schooly!" I blinked, not once but three times. I couldn't believe my eyes.

Dear God, ain't no way You made Schooly this freakin' green. I think You sent him to the wrong family.

This fool had on every stitch of gold that me and Face had jacked off last night. Five rope chains. Rings on every finger. And that ruby-clustered gold watch that the cop was sweatin' this morning.

He had to be crazy.

"Schooly." I ran down the block and rushed up to him. I stood directly in the path of his friends, who caught the bus with him. And no, I didn't say excuse me. Instead, I popped my lips and said, "Montez Carter, why you got that on? Take that mess right back in the house! Now!" I pointed to Da Bricks, and said with a little more edge than I should've. And yeah, I knew I'd embarrassed him, but so what? He didn't need to be walking around wit' the evidence of hot lick. "That's just stupid!"

"Daaaaaaang, you gon' let some girl play you like that?" came from behind my back.

I whipped around and it was some goofy little punk, with a helmet and drooling, all up in my business. "First of all, why you all up in here wit' it?" I sliced my hand across my neck. "'Cause I'm not talking to you, I'm talking to my brother. Now step off." I turned back toward Schooly and the veins in his neck bulged. I started to yank the chains off of him. I settled for yankin' his good arm, and pullin' him to the side. Schooly opened his mouth to speak and a too-big diamond grill fell out. I kicked it into the street.

Before he could say anything I spat, "I'ma cop you dead

in the face if you don't take the rest of that back in the house!"

"And you know Queenie will kick yo' behind if you do! You gave this to me and now you wanna tell me when I can and can't wear it. I'm older than you. You do what I tell you to do."

"You might be older than me, but you acting like a crackhead baby gone wild. If them fools or one of they peoplez see you with they jewelry on, Queenie and Daddy gon' be dropping you in the ground next week! Now take it off!"

"Excuse me, young lady," Schooly's bus driver said, "but he needs to board the bus."

I ignored her. "Take that off, Schooly!"

Schooly looked at me, grabbed his crotch with his good hand, and said, "Eat it. Now step off before you get handled." Then he brushed me to the side and walked onto his bus. A few moments later they took off and disappeared into the distance.

"Yoooooooo." Yvette walked up behind me, sounding just like a surprised Nana. "Oh my God. I can't believe it."

"You holding out on us," Munch insisted. "Why you ain't tell us that Schooly is thugged out now?"

"Straight gangster," Cali agreed.

"We in the last days," Yvette said as we walked down the street to school. "'Cause Schooly need Jesus."

10

Don't stop the rock

I was like a ticking time bomb. Waiting for the moment when I was 'bout to lose it. But I did my best to keep it together. I knew if I flipped and got suspended again, Queenie was gon' uphold her promise to bring her belt to school and beat me in front of er'body.

And word is bond, given the way that I felt—boiling hot, chest huffed up, eyes on fire—if Queenie put her hands on me today I was gon' hit her back.

So, instead of taking that chance, I tried to keep quiet in class and the most I said was, "Present," when the teachers took attendance.

At lunch, I didn't say more than two words to my crew. The nerves in my stomach danced too much. Plus I was beggin' God to not let the cops beat Face up, set him up, or dig up some bogus charges just to keep him down.

And then Schooly...

My fist involuntarily clinched.

Truthfully, I just wanted to rake his behind across the concrete. I hated I even gave him that jewelry. God-lee. He worked my nerves, but he was like my big and little brother, all in one. And the last thing I wanted was for something to happen to him.

He was hardheaded though.

Didn't listen.

And now I had to be on pins and needles looking out for him.

Hopefully, Daddy'll come home tonight and maybe he'll talk some sense into him. And if that don't work, maybe Queenie'll beat the brakes off of him until he has no choice but to understand that this is not a game.

And Jesus pleeeeeeaaaaaaaase let Face be home when I get there.

Amen.

"Excuse me, Miss Carter, but are you going to solve the problem? Or are you not here with us today?"

I blinked twice as my teacher Ms. Jamison's voice brought me out of my thoughts.

My eyes scanned the classroom.

Algebra.

Last period.

Ms. Jamison continued, "Do you hear me speaking to you?"

Blank. Stare.

Don't say nothin'. Not one word. Just chill.

I cocked my neck to the side and sucked my bottom lip into my mouth. I was tryna to nix off the oohs and slips of giggles coming from my classmates.

The teacher folded her arms across her chest. Seems she couldn't leave well enough alone. "Given that you elected to come to school, one would think you'd show up to pay attention."

Don't say nothin'. Not one word.

"Or are you not answering the question because you don't know the answer?"

The whole class laughed. And now I *had* to cuss her out.

I propped both elbows on my desk and leaned forward. But before I could cut her up and serve her, I looked at the problem on the board, solved it in my head, and said, "N equals six times five and X equals nine squared. And your mouth is about to equal you gettin' cussed out."

"Ooh!" the girl next to me blurted out and then slapped a hand over her mouth.

I carried on, "See, I was tryin' not to say nothin' to you, but you don't know how to shut up and I don't know who you think you talkin' to."

"Out of my classroom!"

"Lady, spare me. I didn't even do anything to you. You the one all in my grill. How about this: teach your class and step off 'cause I ain't goin' nowhere. Not today I ain't."

"If you do not leave, I will be calling security!"

"Call 'em."

"And I will be calling your mother."

"Do it. So she can cuss you out, again."

The class was all the way live now, and er'body, with the exception of a few kids in the front and the dude sitting next to me, laughed loudly and egged me on.

I could feel angry tears building in the back of my throat. Dang! I swear, I hated this bird. She worked er'one of my nerves. Every day she went outta her way to say something nasty or call on me for nothing.

Whatever. I couldn't keep sweatin' that, 'cause if I did, this day would be endin' with me hoppin' outta my chair and draggin' this blond-haired ho by her black roots.

Before I could see if this heifer was gon' push me to

take it there, the bell rang and everyone jumped out of their seats. Ms. Jamison yelled something about being suspended, as me and er'body else rushed out of the classroom.

On my way down the hallway, most of my classmates gave me props, but I didn't care. School was over and I just wanted to be up and outta here.

Yvette waited for me at my locker. I tossed my backpack inside of it and we jetted out the door.

"You a'ight?" Yvette asked as we met up with the rest of our crew. They was outside and leaning against a stop sign.

"I'm good. Just hate that the cops took Face."

"Me too."

"I hope he's home when I get there."

"He will be," she said with no sincerity, like she was just talking to be talking.

"You good, homie?" Cali asked as we walked up the block toward Da Bricks. "You was real quiet at lunch."

"I'm straight…" I said, as my voice drifted and I found myself stopping dead in my tracks and stuck in my spot. Munch ran into my back and stepped on the heels of my sneakers, as I watched a silver Audi 5000, the same exact car that me and Face had licked off, bust a U-turn in the street and creep along the sidewalk. I didn't recognize the driver or the passenger.

The passenger hung out the window, and yelled, " 'Ey, yo."

I looked over and I knew freakin' well this one-blue-eyed and one-brown-eyed creep wasn't talkin' to me.

Munch curled her top lip. "Eww. Oh no, you didn't." She shoved both hands up on her hips. "And who is you?"

"And what is you doin'?" Yvette sucked her teeth. "We

don't need no samples and we got our own smoke. Now move along."

The dudes ignored them, pointed to me, and said, "Yo, you Isis?"

I swallowed and hoped the nerves in my stomach didn't tickle my throat and cause my voice to tremble. "Why?" I rocked my neck.

The dudes smiled and light snickers slipped outta their mouths. "Yeah, umm hmm," they said, as if I'd just confirmed what they wanted to know. "Goddamn, girl, I heard about you."

I looked them up and down and hit 'em with death stare. "What? You better get outta my face! I don't care whatchu heard."

The passenger continued, "It's cool though. But hear me on this: let your brother know that we'll be back. Tick. Tick."

I spazzed and flared my arms in the air. "Yo, my man, what you say?! Is that supposed to be a threat?! Do you know who my brother is? Do you know what he'll do to you? Don't get put to sleep, homie."

The passenger answered with a smile and a soft wink while the driver did a U-ey and broke off down the street.

"What the heck was that about?" That was either Munch or Cali, 'cause they both had raspy voices. I couldn't tell which one because I'd taken off running and zooming back to Da Bricks.

Once I broke into my building, I skipped the elevator and instead hopped two steps at a time. After I unlocked our apartment door, I slung it open and rushed to Schooly and Face's room.

Face's bed was empty.

Schooly looked at me and smiled. He was sitting at the head of his bed, back against the wall and proudly draped in hot gold, smacking on a Squirrel Nut candy. He stuck his finger in his mouth and pulled out the hard caramel stuck between his teeth. "What's wrong witchu?"

I shrugged. "Face home?"

"Nope," he said like nothing else mattered but the sticky caramel on his fingertip. "Queenie told Pops that Face had some warrants. And Pops said Face gon' have to sit down for a while."

I felt like somebody had just kicked me in the gut.

"Lil sis, you still mad at me?" Schooly popped another candy in his mouth.

"Yup."

"I thought so. That's why I traded one of those gold necklaces for a box of Chick-O-Sticks. So you wouldn't be mad anymore." He smiled and I promise you I wanted to slam him in his mouth, but I couldn't. So I pushed away the urge and flopped down on the bed next to him.

An *ABC Afterschool Special* was on TV and usually I loved to watch 'em. But the unwanted and unneeded tears that filled the brims of my eyes was in my way. And just when I thought that maybe I could hold them back, they tipped over the edge and fell down my cheeks.

Schooly stretched an arm over my shoulders and pulled my head along the side of his neck. "I'm sorry I told you to eat it. And check it, if you want, and if it means that much to you, I'll take everything off. 'Cept the watch. 'Cause I really like it."

I wiped these dumb tears from my eyes and said, "A'ight, I'll let you rock wit' the watch."

11

Express yourself...

Six months later

A lot had changed.
The year was now 1986.
Spring.
I was thirteen.
And I was no longer checkin' for Doug E. Fresh like that. I had a new love, Eric B., and he wanted to be president.
Daddy no longer came home. And on the nights he wasn't drunk and laid out in the streets, he stayed with Ms. Brenda, her three kids, and the two babies they had together. Daddy tried to come back to Queenie once...scratch that. He tried to come back twice. But, both times Queenie cussed him out, in the middle of the courtyard, and told er'body she'd had enough.
The Down South boys had the juice. They took advantage of Face being gone and was now runnin' Newark streets like they owned them.

My boobs went from a lightweight A-cup to a championship D.

My booty had lifted up where it belonged and was now full. Round. Bounce worthy.

My hair. I switched it up, and no longer let my sun-dyed curls dance everywhere. Now I wore my hair bone straight and let it drape over my shoulders.

Some things was still the same though.

Schooly still rocked that watch. Er'day. All day.

My crew was still my crew. Yvette acted a little funny and had gotten kinda fat. But so what, she was still my homie.

Munch still lived with her country and out-of-date Cousin Shake.

And no matter how she spoke, how she acted, how well she could jump double Dutch, or how many frizzy cornrows she tried to rock, Cali was still white. Period.

My crush was still the same: K-Rock. And I prayed to sweet baby Jesus that since Face was coming home today that K-Rock was on his way over here soooooooon. Real soon.

"Isis!" Queenie called my name and pushed my room door open at the same time. Me and my crew was all gathered on my bed, drooling over the pictures in a *Word Up* magazine.

We looked over at Queenie as she slapped a thigh and said, "Y'all come on out here and help me finish laying this food out in the living room. K-Rock just called and said he and Face is on they way. And folks is already arriving, so come on. I need y'all help." She turned on her heels and rushed out of the doorway.

We all hopped up from the bed and hurried into the

kitchen. Queenie had food everywhere: fried chicken, baked chicken, barbecue turkey wings, ham, fried whiting, cabbage with neck bones, candied yams, cornbread, and chocolate cake.

By the time we'd carried the food out of the kitchen and set it up in the living room, Marvin Gaye was on the turntable and the apartment was filled with people, most of 'em who lived right here in Da Bricks.

"Here they come! Shhhhhhh!" Queenie said in an excited whisper as she flicked the light off.

The living room was bathed in afternoon darkness and everyone was frozen in their spots. K-Rock's and Face's voices echoed from behind the door, as one of them placed their hand on the knob, jiggled it, and then pushed it open.

"SURPRISE! WELCOME HOME!" everybody yelled.

Queenie flicked the light on, and everybody in the room took turns hugging Face. Afterwards, they dug straight into the food.

I tried my hardest to stop blushing, so that I could finally lift my eyes and look over at my future husband.

Okay... breathe in... breathe out...

You can do it. You can do it.

Suck your stomach in.

Stand up straight.

Take a piece of your hair and twirl it with a finger.

Take another deep breath.

Lick your lips so they shine.

Now turn and face him.

Smile.

I almost passed out 'cause the moment I turned around, K-Rock's eyes locked into mine.

Oh my God. Oh my God. Breathe. Breathe.

I grabbed Cali's hand and quickly spun back around, forcing her to twirl with me.

"What the heck? What's wrong with you?" she asked in a panic, her eyes revealing that she was ready to give it to whoever was bringing noise my way.

"It's nothing like that. Chill."

"So what is it?"

"You see that guy standing over there next to Face?"

She almost looked over her shoulder, but I caught her in time. "No! Don't turn around. Not now. He's looking this way."

"Who's looking this way?"

"K-Rock."

She squinted. "K-Rock? Who is that?"

"He used to clock with Face, but when Face got locked up, he fell back a lil bit."

"Okay, so what about him?"

"He's standing over there."

"Can I look now?"

I pulled in and pushed out two deep breaths. "Yes. But turn around slowly."

Cali eased her head around, looked over her shoulder, and then looked back over at me. "He's not over there."

"What?!" My heart dropped and my eyes popped. "What do you mean? Where is he?"

"Right behind you."

My knees buckled and my legs turned to twigs. I squeezed Cali's hand tighter as I eased back around and looked K-Rock dead in his face. "Hey." I gave him a small wave.

"Icy." He reached out for a hug, pulled me into his embrace, and kissed me on my forehead.

Oh God, his lips were soft and so smooth. I wanted sooooooo badly to ask him, practically beg him to kiss me again.

He took a step back and looked me over. His soft brown eyes reflected my hair, my neon-pink fitted mini dress and matching pumps. "Look at you." He smiled and gave me another once over. "All grown up."

"I'm thirteen now." I knew I sounded super stupid.

"How old are you?" Cali butted in and I had to do a double take. Just that quick I'd forgotten she was standing there.

"Seventeen," he said, proudly.

Cali blushed. "All right now, girl. I see you like an older man."

My stomach hit the floor and my heart went right behind it. I looked at Cali like she was completely crazy.

She bit into her bottom lip. "I'm sorry. I was just excited."

I ignored her apology and turned back to K-Rock. "She's crazy. Anyway, wassup with you? I ain't seen you in a minute."

"Yeah, I know. Been laying low. But it's cool now...."

I knew he was talking, but I was no longer listening. I was too busy taking in his beautiful skin, light beard, white tee, MCM jacket, chocolate-colored Levi's, and crisp white Reeboks.

I imagined him reaching for my hand and asking me to dance. After all, Queenie just had Schooly drop the needle on Meli'sa Morgan's "Do Me Baby." And God knows I was dying to be done.

Do me, K-Rock. Do. Me. Please.

"You wanna dance, baby?" shook me from my daydream.

I blinked and focused in on K-Rock. There was a tall, super skinny, and caramel-colored chick standing next to him. He placed his arm around her waist and said, "Hold up, baby I want you to meet my lil sis, Icy. Icy, this is Shakira. My girlfriend."

Girlfriend? Really?

Word?

I felt like the dumbest chick on Earth. All I wanted to do at this moment was catch a rocket and get outta here.

So this is what he's really been doing—chillin' with this bird.

I glanced over at Cali and, judging by her curled top lip, she was just as pissed and surprised as I was.

I put on the stankest face that I could muster up and said, "My name is *I. Sis. Isis.* Not Icy. Do not call me that." I shot K-Rock a cruddy look. "I told you that before. And he is *not* my big brother."

K-Rock gave me a crooked grin, shook his head, and said, "You buggin'." He flicked my chin. "Cute. But bugged."

Shakira didn't open her mouth and it was a good thing she didn't because that would've been the excuse I needed to bust her in it. She gave me a phony smile though.

I left them standing there and walked over to Face, as Cali walked over and kicked it with our crew.

Face sipped a glass of fruit punch and his eyes scanned the room.

I stood next to him and leaned against the wall. His eyes never stopped scanning the crowd as he said, "I missed you, lil sis."

"I missed you too. Did you get the letters I sent you?"

"Yeah. I got all of 'em. Now I want you tell me again what them dudes said when they rolled up on you. I want

K-Rock to hear it." He looked over at K-Rock and mo-
tioned for him to come over to us. He did, minus the
chick. I still rolled my eyes though. Anything to keep from
blushing. Face looked taken aback as he looked from me
to K-Rock and back again. "Tell me again," Face continued.

I folded my arms across my chest. "Yo, I was with my
crew, walking home from school and that same Audi that we
ran through pulled up. It wasn't the same dudes though."

"How they look?" Face asked.

"I couldn't see the driver that good, but the passenger,
who was doing all the talking, was light skin with two
different-color eyes. One brown and one blue."

"That's Snoop." K-Rock nodded. "A'ight." He nodded
again. "So repeat what they said."

I continued, "They was like, 'You Isis?' "

"And what you say?" Face pressed.

"I said, 'Why? Who wanna know?' "

"And then what?" K-Rock asked.

"They said, 'Tell yo' brother we coming back. Tick.
Tick.' "

K-Rock arched his brow. "Oh, word?"

"Word," I confirmed.

"A'ight." Face resumed sipping his drink. "Straight. We
got it from here."

He and K-Rock exchanged dap, and then K-Rock returned to his bird.

"Face," I said. "Maybe you should lay low for a while?
You just got home. I'm not saying be no punk. I'm just saying maybe you should chill for a minute. You see things is
different. Daddy ain't here no more and them Down
South boys runnin' the block."

"Pops ain't never really been here. And them boys runnin' the block, for now. Only for now. But you don't need to worry about that."

"I'm just saying you need to lay back and observe before you make a move. I don't want anything happen to you."

He smiled. "I'm good, lil sis. And don't tell me you growing up and turning into a mushy lil chick on me."

I whipped around and faced him completely. "What you talking about? Don't play me." My eyes drifted as K-Rock walked by with his ho.

Face laughed. "You still got a crush on him?"

I couldn't believe he said that. "What? Me? Ill? Ain't *noooooooobody* thinking about him but his lil ugly broad. I couldn't care less."

"I bet."

"Anywho, let's get back to you. Chill. Just for a minute."

"Trust me, lil sis." He leaned off the wall and his eyes burned through a chubby Yvette as she carried a plate of food and sat down in a chair. "Ain't nothing gon' happen to me. I'ma always be here." And then he walked away and left me standing there.

12

Makes me wonder

I dreamed I was covered in blood and drowning. Something was pulling me under.

I couldn't breathe. I couldn't move. I couldn't scream. I couldn't wake up.

I was held hostage in my bed, paralyzed.

By the time I'd snatched myself out of my sleep, I was on edge.

And that's exactly how I felt all day.

Which is why I'd snapped on er'body.

Anybody who came in my path caught it.

And the first sucker I served was Face. He bolted into my room early this morning, asking me to cuss out some stalkin' hoochie he couldn't shake.

Then I had to slay Schooly for once again drapin' himself in every piece of gold that he owned.

And by the time I got to school I had to give it to my crew.

Yvette got it 'cause she complained *allllllll* through homeroom about her back and stomach hurting.

Munch caught it because she complained *alllllllll* through history class about Yvette's back and stomach hurting too much.

And Cali got handled 'cause she cornered me, in-between classes, to drop the science that the last time her stomach hurt like Yvette's she was pregnant.

"You need to go to the doctor," I said to Yvette, after school, as we walked down the hall to my apartment. "'Cause I'm sick of you complaining. All day. Every day." We walked into my room and she huffed as she sat down on my bed.

"I don't need to see no doctor," she said like I had lost my mind.

"Oh yes, you do." I pulled a bag of weed from my night-stand drawer and dumped the contents on the back of an album cover.

"I just need something to calm my nerves that's all." She opened the pack of EZ Wider, rolled a joint, and sparked it up. "Nana's been buggin' a lot lately." She took a pull and then passed me the joint.

I lay back against the wall, closed my eyes, and took the longest pull that I could. And just as I let the smooth herb soak into my lungs, I heard Yvette gagging. "Yvette!" I screamed. She was bent over the side of my bed, dry heaving. "What the...!" I mashed the joint in the ashtray. "Do I need to call Nana? Nine-one-one?"

She sucked her teeth. "No. I think it's the flu or something." She managed to stand up. "I'm going downstairs to get in my bed. I don't feel too good." She took a step and stumbled.

"What is wrong with you?" I helped her sit down.

"Just my stomach."

"You constipated?" I said, taking a wild guess.

"Maybe." She shrugged.

"Okay. Well, just lay down on my bed and I'ma send Schooly to the store to get a ginger ale for your stomach." I took fifty cents from my drawer and hurried out of my room. "Schools! Schooly!" I ran to his room and opened the door. "School—" I hesitated.

He wasn't there.

Bed still was made from this morning.

And the TV wasn't on.

I walked back into the hallway and peeped into each room. No Schooly. Which pissed me off all over again, because he knew Queenie didn't let him go nowhere without telling somebody where he was going.

"Now I got to hear Queenie's mouth," I grumbled, walking out the apartment door, "if his butt is not home when she gets there. Ugg!"

"Where you goin'?" Cali yelled out, as I stepped out of the building and into the courtyard. She hopped off the back of the park bench and walked alongside me to the store.

"First, I'm going to run up in here to get Yvette a ginger ale for her stomach and then I'm going to find Schooly. His butt was not in his room and he knows Queenie don't let him roam like that. And after the day I've had, I do not need Queenie in my face blaming me for Schooly doing some dumbness."

"I just saw Schooly." Cali handed me a C&C ginger ale out of the cooler.

I set the soda and two quarters on the counter. Then I looked at her and frowned. "You just saw Schooly? Whatchu mean? Where at?" The cashier placed the soda and a straw in a brown paper bag and handed it to me.

As we walked out of the store and crossed the street,

Cali continued, "Matter fact, I saw him in the store about thirty minutes ago, buying some Squirrel Nuts and two Chick-O-Sticks."

"Did you see where he went after that?"

She nodded. "Yeah. He saw somebody he knew and got in the car with 'em."

I stopped in my tracks. "He did what? Schooly?" I looked at Cali, confused. "Are you sure?"

"Yeah."

"He don't know nobody wit' no car. Yo, why you ain't stop him or come and get me?" I snapped, feeling the urge to backhand her.

"'Cause it ain't look like there was a problem. Everything looked copacetic to me. Chill. He just probably went for a ride with one of his friends."

"You sound real dumb right now! He's slow. He don't have no friends who drive or have cars! And anyway what kind of car was it?"

"I don't appreciate you calling me dumb! And it didn't look like a problem to me."

"What kind of car was it?!" I said anxiously, stamping my feet. "Tell me!"

"I didn't really notice the kind of car it was. I know it was silver though."

13

White lines

Six p.m.

It had been three hours, forty-five minutes, and too many seconds to count that I didn't know where Schooly was. And either I needed Schooly home or I needed somewhere to go until he got here.

I crept outta bed, leaving Yvette lying there, and grabbed my boom box. Then I eased through the living room window, sat on the fire escape, and did all I could to focus on Red Alert's *show*, desperately wantin' to rock to the underground artists spittin' freestyles.

But I couldn't.

So I looked down at the old man skin poppin' his johnson in the alleyway.

But I couldn't focus on that either.

"What is you doin' up there?" a chickenhead yelled at me, as she kicked bits of glass and trash with her feet.

"Minding my business."

"I can't tell. 'Cause you look like you all in mines!" She

grabbed a red-haired white man by the hand, gently pushed him against the building, and then slid to her knees.

I shut my eyes and squeezed them extra tight.

God please...

"Isis." Queenie walked in the front door and looked directly at me. She walked over to the open window and stuck her head through. "Whatchu doing out there?"

I swallowed. A million things ran through my mind to tell her.

"I asked you a question," she said, like she'd been waiting on an answer a moment too long.

I shook my head. "Nothing. Just chillin'."

"You chillin' on a fire escape in the middle of Da Bricks? For what? Waitin' for a bullet with no name on it?" She looked at me like I was crazy. "Get off that thing and get back in here. Nobody got time for that. Find something else to do." She turned away and yelled, "Schooly! Schooly! I want you to go to the store and get me a Pepsi!"

My heart thundered. "He ain't here." I climbed back into the living room, boom box in tow.

The look in her eyes clearly asked me where he was.

Think. Think. Think. "He's with Face."

"And where they go?"

I hunched my shoulders. "I don't know. They didn't tell me."

"I don't believe this. I always like an ice-cold Pepsi while I'm bagging up weed."

"You want me to get it?"

"You know damn well you don't go to nobody's store at night." She furrowed her brow. "What is wrong witchu?"

"Nothin'."

She looked at me suspiciously and then snatched my

chin. "Your dang daddy been by here? Did you let him in here? Is he here now? I told you he is not allowed to come back here!"

"No." I yanked my chin away. "I ain't seen Daddy."

She paused. Soaked this in a moment and then said, "Well then go find something to do 'cause you acting crazy."

Eight p.m.

I sat on the edge of my bed with my knees folded into my chest and my face buried in my thighs. Trying my best to stay focused on Schooly coming home and not thinking the worst.

Yvette had fallen asleep on the side of my bed, holding her stomach and moaning every ten minutes. Truthfully, I wanted to put her out, but I knew she had to be in real pain to not wanna knock off the rest of this joint with me.

So I left her alone and let her sleep.

I hopped off the bed, lit about five Black Love incenses in here, and lined the bottom of my door with a towel. Hoping and praying Queenie wouldn't smell the weed. The last thing I needed was her spazzing on me about getting zooted or realizing that one of her nickel bags was missin'.

Ten p.m.

I wished I could stop pacing.

I just wanted to close my eyes and sit still. But I couldn't.

Face hadn't come back yet.

And I needed him to come back.

Soon.

Queenie bolted into my room. "Where did you say Face and Schooly went?"

I froze. Then dropped my eyes to the floor. "I don't know."

I could feel her staring at me. "You don't know? You don't know? I tell you what, Face better hurry back up in here with my boy. Got my nerves on edge. And wake Yvette up. She needs to go home."

She closed the door behind her and I felt like I wanted to disappear.

Midnight.
I could hear Queenie walking the living room floor.
Still no Face.
And no Schooly.

One a.m.
I'd fallen asleep and my dreams made me feel like I was drowning again. That something was pulling me under.
I couldn't move.
And I couldn't scream.
I felt trapped.
I couldn't breathe.
I needed to breathe.
I felt my arms flailing in the air, but I still couldn't wake up. Then suddenly, as if someone had slugged me in the back of my head I sat straight up and screamed, "Schooly!"

Two a.m.
No Schooly.
Yvette is pissing in my bed.
And Queenie keeps questioning me every five minutes.

Four a.m.
Yvette is calling on Jesus, and Queenie is yelling for me.

"Get up!" Queenie pounded and jiggled the knob on my locked bedroom door. I hopped out of bed and ran out into the hallway, closing the door behind me.

"What?" I said in a panic. "Is Schooly home?"

"No!" she said, her eyes bloodshot red with worry. "The cops is back and they must have a warrant this time!" She rushed into the kitchen and I ran behind her, repeating the routine, over and over again in my head.

Get the work!
The guns!
And the cash.
Dump 'em in a trash bag!
Run to the roof!
Repeat.
Get the work!
The guns!
And the cash.
Dump 'em in a trash bag!
Run to the roof!
Repeat!

"Come on!" Queenie snapped as she emptied clips from the two guns she had and tossed them in a trash bag. "Load the stash!"

I did as I was told and, once the bag was full, Queenie pushed me toward the back door. I ran to the roof and hid the goods. But instead of waiting on the roof like I was s'pose to, I came back downstairs, cracked the back door open, and looked to see if the police had the front door on the floor and Queenie handcuffed.

They didn't.

Two officers, dressed in navy-blue trousers, white shirts, and khaki trench coats, flashed their badges and the lead officer said, "Mrs. Beverly Carter?"

Queenie swallowed. Nobody ever called her by her government name.

She shoved a hand up on her hip and said, tight-lipped, "Who wanna know?"

"You mind if we come in?" the officer asked.

"Oh, you will not be comin' up in here without no warrant."

"We're not here to search your place, ma'am. We're from homicide, and your son—"

Her eyes scanned their faces. She sucked her teeth and sighed in exhaustion. "Ezekiel Jr. ain't here."

The officer shook his head. "No, ma'am. I'm here to speak to you about your other son, Montez Carter. His body was found on the McCarter Highway bridge...."

14

Close to the edge

Two weeks later

"They forgot about me," I whispered to Yvette as I sat at my nana's small and round kitchen table, my eyes tracing the aged grease spots splattered behind the stove.

"Who forgot about you?"

I turned around and stared at Yvette. Her hair was sticking straight up on the top of her head. Dark circles seemed to eat up her eyes, as she squinted and looked straight through me.

"Whatchu mean?" she asked, placing the baby that she'd delivered in my bed, the same day Schooly died, on her shoulder.

"All of 'em. Queenie—"

"Yo, where she go?" Yvette asked, like she'd been dying to know that.

"I don't know." I shrugged. "After the funeral she told

me she was going to the store to get herself a Pepsi. That was two weeks ago."

"You think Uncle Zeke know where she is?"

I rolled my eyes and rocked my neck. "Psst. Please. Spare me. He don't know nothing, except what Ms. Brenda tell him."

"What about Face?"

"He in the streets somewhere. I guess laying low. The last time I saw him was at Schooly's funeral. Afterwards, he told me he was gon' find the dude, Snoop. I haven't seen him since."

She shook her head.

"You know what I've been thinking," I said.

"What?"

"That I might go back upstairs to my old apartment and wait for Face and Queenie. I hate it here."

Yvette grunted and let out a slight chuckle.

That pissed me off.

She smacked her lips. "Girl, please. Some crackheads broke in your old apartment and stole everything they could. I saw somebody walkin' out with the sink yesterday."

"What?! You watched 'em do that?!"

"And what did you expect me to do? Who I look like to you? Five-oh? Not."

"Whatever! It's cool 'cause Face gon' come back and find us someplace else to live. Da Bricks ain't the last place on Earth."

"Yeah, okay. You keep waiting on Face."

"And whatchu mean by that?" I snapped. "You know you pushin' your luck, right? You know I'm not in the mood for no BS, right? You know I'm 'bout to go *alllll* the way off, right? And I don't know what or who has pissed you off. Maybe it was your baby daddy, but I don't know and I don't care. So, I suggest you watch yo' mouth and be easy when you talkin' to me."

Yvette paused and an awkward silence filled the room. After a few minutes, she said, "I was in the courtyard yesterday and er'body saying Face found that dude who killed Schooly."

I swallowed the lump that forced its way in my throat. "I hope he did and I hope his mama droppin' flowers on 'im."

Yvette sat down and lay the baby across her lap. "Well, just in case nobody comes back for you, I'm tellin' you now, all Nana gon' do is feed you. That's it. Don't look for no clothes. You not about to be fly, not off of Nana's dime, anyway. You ain't gon' rock no hotness. And you gon' always hate it here." She shook her head. "Always. And whatever you do," she whispered as we heard footsteps approach the kitchen, "don't let Stick get to you. She like to mess with er'body."

Yvette's two little brothers and sister ran into the kitchen and grabbed bowls for their cereal, while my twenty-year-old aunt, Evelyn, who er'body called Stick, 'cause all her life she'd been way too skinny, pushed her boney hips through the crowded kitchen. "Just the two I wanna see."

"Why?" I twisted my lips.

She slammed the *Star Ledger* over my bowl of cereal, then leaned against the stove and smiled. "You see Face right?"

I soaked in Face's picture and the headline: NEWARK DRUG DEALER ARRESTED FOR EXECUTION-STYLE MURDER. My eyes scrolled further down into the article. *It is believed that Carter's victims may have killed his brother....*

My breath was short. My heart raced and rushed into

my throat, and a few seconds later, it exploded. I tried to swallow the pieces before anybody noticed.

I failed.

Tears rushed to my eyes and er'body was starin' at me.

Stick carried on, "You know it's over for him, right? You know he 'bout to do football numbers, right?" She popped her black ashy lips.

I did my best to contain my tears. *Just chill.* "You need to go 'head with that. Always tryna front on somebody."

"Psst, please." Stick laughed. "You can't front on the truth. And anyway I'm grown. I can say what I wanna say 'cause you in my house, lil girl."

"Yo' house? This is Nana's house!" My eyes scanned the kitchen and mostly er'body except Yvette was gigglin'.

My blood boiled and rushed up my back.

Five . . . four . . . three . . .

I couldn't believe this. . . . Face was in jail. . . .

In jail . . .

For murder . . .

How was I gon' get outta here now?

If I stayed here much longer, I was gon' bug out.

For one: Fifty-eleven fools ran through Nana's apartment on a regular.

And two: There was only two bedrooms in here. Nana slept in one and too many people slept in the other one.

I had no idea who lived here, who was layin' low, or who was just visitin'. There was no space to have your own space. No room to think. No room to chill. All you could do up in here was exist. That's it.

"Like I said, go 'head." I managed to blink back tears.

Stick smirked. "And if I *don't?*"

"All right now," Nana yelled into the kitchen. "It's too

early for foolishness! Y'all talkin' too loud and Bill is back there tryna get some sleep!"

I ignored Nana's warnin' and said, "First of all, Stick, why you all in my business?" I cocked my neck to the left. "You need to slow down. At least my brother took care of me. But you? Don't nobody take care of you. You assed out. Assed out in the face. Assed out in the body. It's only a matter of time before you pimped out and beatin' that concrete, you baldheaded fiend! Now you better get outta my face and back up before you get smacked up."

Stick laughed. "Smacked up? I double dare you. Mess around and get put over my lap, lil girl. Face can't save you now and yo' mama and daddy don't care nothin' about you!"

I looked over at Yvette and she mouthed, *Forget her.*

And she was right—I needed to forget her.

But I couldn't.

You let some hos disrespect you? I'ma peel the high-yellah black offa you.

Suddenly, I felt like I was back on the playground and standin' in front of Aiesha again. And just like on the playground, if I let Stick get off wit' dissin' me, then er'body in the kitchen was gon' think they could bring it to me. Whenever. Wherever.

I stood up from the table and just as Stick carried on about how Queenie was a ho, I reached for a half-empty forty beer bottle that somebody had left on the table and bashed Stick dead in the face. The bottle exploded and jagged pieces of wet glass rained er'where. Stick screamed and blood spurted from her face onto Nana's yellow walls like wild red paint.

15

Planet Rock

The afternoon

"Itold you not to do that." Yvette handed me a plastic
bag filled with ice. I smacked it away and ice scattered
all over the peeling linoleum floor.

She placed the baby in her bassinet and then curled up
next to me in bed. For once, we were the only three in the
room. Yvette leaned into my ear and whispered, "Told you
to forget Stick."

I sighed and my swollen eyes soaked in the five twin-
sized beds and piles of clothes in here. This was hell. It
had to be. There was no TV. No posters. One white and one
red bedsheet tacked over the window. Pockets of holes
punched in the walls. And dirty stuffed animals everywhere.

"I wish you had listened to me." Yvette looked over her
shoulder at me and shook her head. "You just straight lost
it. Totally tripped."

"So? And? I'm not no sucka, and unlike you, they ain't

'bout to talk to me any kind of way and treat me crazy; 'cause I will bring the noise. And anyway, I will not let no ho disrespect me. Aunt or no aunt."

"You need to learn how to shut up sometimes."

"And you need to learn to speak up. If anything, you should've been helpin' me."

"Help you? And get me *annnnd* my baby put out. We don't have nowhere else to go! This is it for me!"

"How they gon' all jump me? It shoulda been a fair one."

Her eyes grew wide. "How you figure that? You slaughtered Stick in the face wit' a bottle!"

"So?! And?! That wasn't no reason for Uncle Chuck to run in there and snatch me by the back of my neck and hold me down. All so Stick could bolo my face."

I carried on, "Then you just stand there lookin' stupid. And Nana." I shuddered, suckin' up snot. "She gon' whip me with an extension cord. What kind of grandmother does that?! Huh? All these welts on my legs. That fat tramp. I hope when she goes outside she gets flattened by a truck. Old slut. That's why my daddy hated her, and me too! Wait till I tell Queenie!"

"Queenie don't care!"

"Yes, she does!"

"No, she doesn't and you know it, and she ain't comin' back. So you may as well stop lookin' for her."

If my mouth wasn't sore, I woulda cussed Yvette out like the punk broad she was, but I let it go and lay there feelin' like somebody had sliced opened my heart and pissed on the inside.

A few minutes into feeling sorry for myself, Nana stormed into the bedroom. Her bare brown feet slapped the floor with every step she took. She grunted and shoved a hand up on her wide hip. The plastic cap she had her Jheri curl tucked in rustled with her every movement. She folded her hands over her large and droopin' breasts and belted, "Being high yellow wit' good hair don't earn you no special privileges up in here."

This fat tramp was stupid. "What?"

"Don't what me! Now, I don't know who you think you is, but you lucky I didn't beat you in the face with a beer bottle so you would know how it felt!"

Silence.

She carried on, "Obviously, you got this twisted: I'm not your drunk daddy or your missing mama. I don't owe you nothing and I don't have to put up with your foolishness. Now if you wanna be put outta here, end up in some lil group home, or find yourself dead right along there with Schooly, act a fool up in here again and watch what happens to you."

She looked over at Yvette. "And you already know that you on your last whorin' behind leg. You better thank God that I told my son that I would help him and yo' mama out. Up there having babies. And if I find out that you was messin' wit' some old-tail man, I will call the cops on him, and he will be going to jail."

More silence.

Nana carried on, "Now, Isis, I know your mama and daddy didn't have any rules, which is why you and your brothers ended up the way you did, but I got some. Rule number one: Every. Body. In here is outta the bed by seven a.m. Period."

Seven?

"Seven," she snapped. " 'Cause the only thing asleep after seven in the mornin' is junkies and whores."

I looked at this old broad like she was nuts.

Nana frowned. "You look at me like that again and I'ma slap the hellfire from you."

I turned away and twisted my lips.

"Rule number two: No stealin'. Period. Nothin' I hate more than a thief. You want somethin', then you better find you a lil job or a lil grind. 'Cause allowing you to live here—rent free—is all you gon' get from me. Understand?" She paused, as if she expected me to answer. "You testin' me?" she snapped.

I sucked my teeth but refused to answer.

"Answer me when I'm talkin' to you!" she screamed in my face. "You will respect me 'cause I'm not your lil girl-friend!"

I know you not my girlfriend 'cause if you were I woulda slapped you.

"Do you hear me?!" she screamed.

I felt like taking it to her throat and puttin' a bolo right in her face.

Nana took a step closer to me. "Answer. Me."

I did everything I could to hold back tears, but just as I went to say something, anything...they streamed down my face.

Nana sucked her teeth and shook her head at me. "After all the hell you raised up in here this morning, now you wanna cry?" She looked over at Yvette. "Help your cousin get herself together. And then y'all get in that kitchen and clean up that glass and wash that blood off my wall!"

16

Summertime

Two months later

Ninety degrees.
Sweltering hot.

School was out.

The sun was scorching er'thing and er'body in sight.

The Down South boys had completely taken over and half of Da Bricks was they trap houses.

People who'd lived here forever was movin' out by the busloads.

There was rumors going around that City Hall was trying to open a shopping complex over here, had scheduled Da Bricks for demolition, and would be relocatin' er'body.

Didn't really matter to me 'cause I felt like er'thing had already been knocked down. And besides, all I wanted to do was run away. But I couldn't think of nowhere to go, especially since I'd never been outside of Newark, unless riding through Irvington counted for something.

Queenie was still missin'.

Face was still in jail.

And although er'night I dreamed Schooly was alive, by mornin' I always remembered he was dead, and that it was sorta my fault.

My love for hip-hop was buried inside the black hole in my chest. And I hadn't heard no song nor seen no rap-daddy who made me want to reincarnate it.

All I could see from where I was sittin' on Nana's rusty fire escape overlooking the courtyard, was that I didn't have nothin' and it wasn't gon' change.

"How long you gon' be mad?" Yvette popped her lips, as she stuck her head through the window, interrupting my moment.

"God-lee," I sighed. "How long you gon' stay sweatin' me?"

"Munch and Cali keep asking me to ask you to please come outside. They miss you, and I do too. And anyway, whatchu mean, God-lee? And I'm not always sweatin' you. You just acting like a real creep right now. I understand that your brother died, but dang, did you die too?!"

"You better step off."

"Why you gotta be mad at the world?"

"I'm not mad at the world. I just don't wanna be bothered wit' nobody. So like I said, step off. And, anyway, maybe I like it out here." I rocked my neck.

"Lies." She twisted her lips. "You know it ain't nothing out here but some fiends, them Down South boys and a few kids. And guess what?"

"What?"

"Guess who I saw noddin' out over by the Dumpster, the other day?"

"Who?"

"Stick."

"Whoopty doo. Whatchu want, a cookie? You shoulda told her fat and stankin' mama since she always got somethin' to say, and see what she had to say about that."

I could tell Yvette was tryna hold back a giggle. "I did tell her."

"And what her big ass do but breathe heavy? 'Cause she can't run."

A snicker slipped out. "You shoulda saw Nana tryin' to run. Man, I like to died! Her breasts was bouncing er'where." Yvette couldn't hold it in any longer and now she was laughing so hard that she was crying. "Nana went behind that Dumpster, dragged Stick out by her hair, and beat her with a belt."

Yvette sat down on the window sill and howled. She could barely breathe as she recapped what she thought were the funniest parts of what happened to Stick. "Yoooooo, you shoulda seen it."

Blank. Stare.

Was she serious? No. She. Could. Not. Be. Serious. Did she really think we was about to toss it up like best friends? She could miss me wit' that. "Girl, boo," I snapped. "You really think I wanna hear about Stick? Puhlease. You already know what time it is. Dismissed."

Yvette looked toward the ceiling and fluttered her lashes. "Oh, I see how this is gon' go. You gon' be mad forever." She yawned. "That pissed-off routine is 'bout to get real tired wit' me."

"Well, then step off and get you some rest 'cause I'ma be mad 'til I feel like bein' glad. So it's no need for you to be all in my grill, tryna act like we homegirls again. 'Cause we're not."

"Dang! Watz yo' dealie-o, yo? Why you all of a sudden actin' like you crazy?"

"Crazy? I act crazy?" I flung my arms up in the air. "But you keep sweatin' me? All I know is that I would've never watched nobody jump you. But you? You stood by and watched Stick, Nana, and Uncle Chuck drag me."

"You tried to kill Stick! And from what I could see, you got what your hand called for. And the same thing they did to you, they would've done for you."

"Psst, please. I don't need none of them to do nuffin' for me. I got this."

"Yeah, and is that why you sittin' on a fire escape over-looking garbage and fiends, 'cause you got it?"

"Whatever. Don't you have a surprise baby to go and feed or somethin'?"

"Don't be tossing that in my face. You must want me to cuss you out and mess you up!"

Cuss me out? Mess me up? I ice grilled her. "Yo, for real, you already know I ain't the one."

"And me either. And you're right, I know what time it is, time to step off and leave your miserable self alone!"

"Then be out."

"I'm out. And when you learn how to act like the old Isis again, my best friend and favorite cousin, then *maybe* we can go and chill with our crew. Or maybe go to Wee-quahic Park. So we can see the B-boys break-dance and bust a freestyle. Maybe even win a break-dancing contest and get another mixtape. But as of right now, since your mind is all tore up, I don't wanna mess you up. So peace." She hit me with two fingers, stuck her head back through the window, and rocked her neck.

I just stared at her. 'Cause the only reason why I didn't

take it to her dome was because clearly she didn't see how a beat down was gon' be the last line of her eulogy. And being that she was now somebody's mama, I let her get that.

I watched her walk away and then I looked back down into the courtyard. Munch and Cali were bopping their heads to somebody's boom box.

I wish it was mine.

"Why you playin' us out?" Munch yelled to me, as she stood up on the park bench and held her head up toward the fire escape.

I flicked a wrist. "Ain't nobody playin' you out. Whatchu talking about?"

"The whole last two months of school, you didn't talk to us. And the last time you chilled with us was so long ago that I can't even remember when. What's really good with that?"

"I got a lot of things on my mind. I can't chill with y'all right now."

"And why not?"

"'Cause I don't want to!"

"We miss you though," Cali added.

"So." I hunched. A part of me missed them too, but the other part of me just wanted to click my heels and hit another dimension.

"Yvette told us you was crazy," Munch said. "And judgin' by how stank you acting, I believe it." She and Cali hopped off the park bench and walked away.

I felt stupid. Lost. Confused. I knew I needed to get up from here and go make up with my crew. But, I wasn't exactly sure how I could live a whole life. A whole one wit' no Queenie. No Face. And a dead Schooly. I didn't even know where to start or what to say.... Hell, I needed to be reintroduced to myself.

I climbed through the window and walked back to the bedroom I shared with everybody except Nana and her boyfriend. My little cousins were stretched across the floor and playing jacks, while Yvette was changing her baby Kamari's Pamper.

Yvette shot me a side eye and then reached for the baby powder.

"So what do you call that, an attitude?" I said.

She ignored me.

"Don't tell me you're mad at me now?" I pressed.

Silence.

I sucked my teeth. "You wanna go chill with the crew today? Maybe go to the park?"

Yvette's eyes lit up, but her mouth twisted to the side. "Nope."

"Well, I wanna go." I walked over to the bed and sat next to her.

"And how we gon' get there? It's too far to walk."

"I thought you ain't wanna go?"

"I don't. I'm just asking."

"We could walk."

"Walk? Psst. Please. Walkin' is played out. Plus I got this baby now. You wanna catch the bus?"

"You got money?"

She looked at me like I had two heads. "No. Nana gave me money to buy Kamari some milk and Pampers. That's it."

"And you know I'm broke."

"So I guess we ain't goin'."

We both leaned back against the bedroom wall and sighed in defeat.

"Dang, I can't take being stuck up in this place another freakin' day," I said.

Yvette stared off into space. Then she seemed to gather her thoughts, as she said, "You really wanna go somewhere today?"

"Yeah. But how we gon' get wherever we goin'?"

"We gon' catch a bus."

I pressed the back of my hand against her forehead. "Are you sick or something? You just heard me say I didn't have any money."

"Look, don't trip. We gon' get some money."

"Oh, word? And where we gon' get the money from?"

"We gon' steal it."

17

Bust a move

"You sure they not gon' wake up?" I said as me and
Yvette stood at Nana's bedroom door and I softly
inched it open, one hand on the knob and the other slapped
over my nose. "Wassup wit' that smell?" I frowned, feeling
like the stench of funky behind, stale Thunderbird, and a
burned crack pipe had bust me in the face.

"What you mean? You been here for two months and
you never noticed that on the weekends Nana and Mr. Bill
tear this room up? She be up in there drunk as I don't
know what and Mr. Bill be in there gettin' beamed up."

"No. I never really noticed that."

"Well, welcome to Nana's world. And that's why we
gon' run up in there real quick and handle our business."

I wasn't so sure I wanted to do this. I'd never been no
petty thief before. And no, stealing hip-hop magazines,
jelly bracelets, and a nickel bag of weed here and there
from the bodega and Queenie didn't count. That shoulda
been free anyway.

But. This was different.

We was desperate.

And I guess desperate times called for standing at your grandmama's door with your eye on her rent drawer.

"Yvette," I whispered, gently pulling the door closed, and turning toward her. "One of her rules was everybody had to be outta the bed by seven a.m. It's almost eight."

"But it's Sunday."

"And? What that mean to me? And anyway, just 'cause you say you wanna rob somebody today don't mean you actually do it today. You gotta watch the joker first. Case they place and see how they move."

"I've been living with Nana for two years."

"Yeah, well, I just got here. And I don't know her Sunday routine and I don't know the easiest way in her bedroom or the smoothest way out."

"What, you scared?" Yvette paused and then looked at me like calling me a punk was at the tip of her tongue.

I looked Yvette up and down. I may have been in a bad spot right now, but I was still thorough and she better know it.

She sighed and then whispered, "Look, trust me. They ain't waking up."

"And what about when she does wake up and realizes her rent money is missing?"

"She gon' accuse him. Beat him up. Drag him. And if he piss her off enough, she might cut him. But she'll patch him up, he'll give her some money, and they'll be back together by next Sunday."

I eyed Yvette suspiciously. Seems she's been movin' like a petty thief for a while now. "And how long you been doing this?"

"What is this, a job interview? You wanna lick the drawer or not?"

I smirked, as I held onto the doorknob, opened the door again, and we both pressed our faces into the crack. Yvette stood on her tippy toes behind me and looked over my head.

Nana slept in a flimsy white and sheer gown. Her wig cap was twisted, revealin' the five jumbo cornrows she had plaited to the back. She lay to the left of her boyfriend, Mr. Bill, who was tucked on the inside of Nana's flabby arm.

"Told you," Yvette whispered. "She ain't gettin' outta that bed today. We might not even see Nana for the whole weekend."

"Okay. So tell me where the money at so I can snatch it real quick."

Yvette planted her feet flat on the floor and tapped me on the shoulder. I turned around and she said, "There you go actin' crazy again. Why would I let you go snatch the money?"

I curled my top lip and swerved my neck. "You tryna play me."

"No. But I'm sayin' you been somebody different for a minute. How I know you back to the old Isis?"

"Oh, word? So this how we getting' down now? You doubtin' me."

She twisted her lips. "Look, I know where the money at and I know how to get in and get outta there. So, I'ma get the money and you gon' be the lookout. And I'm not gettin' ready to argue with you. 'Cause if you really wanna go snatch the money, go get it. But if she does wake up and sees you, just know she gon' call the state on you. And when they drag you outta here, you'll be rollin' to yo' new group home alone. I been in foster care and I ain't goin' back. Now how you wanna do this?"

I took a step back. "You get the money."

"Thought so. Now keep an eye out for Stick, 'cause she likes to breeze through here and I don't need her catchin' us. 'Cause the last time she caught me sneakin' in here she muscled me into givin' her half of the money."

"Well, she ain't gettin' half of nothin' over here."

"Exactly. So watch the door."

Yvette eased into Nana's bedroom, with the grace of a ballerina dancing across the floor. Nana started to rustle, Yvette hit the floor, and I pulled the door, leaving only a slither of space for me to see through.

Nana never opened her eyes, she simply turned over and her naked behind faced the door. I frowned. I'd never seen a booty look so riddled with dents as deep as bullet holes before.

I looked back over to Yvette, who had eased Nana's top dresser drawer open and slid her hand inside. She felt around for a moment and shook her head. She looked back at me and her eyes told me it wasn't there. She checked the other four drawers. Nothing.

Shit.

Nana started to rustle again. Yvette hit the floor and I closed the door.

A few seconds later, Yvette eased out and we hurried back to our bedroom. "She must've moved it. 'Cause it wasn't there," she said.

"Dang."

"Don't sweat it though, 'cause Mr. Bill's wallet was on the nightstand and he had a fifty-dollar bill in there." She popped the bill and stretched it. "So I snatched it and we gon' split it."

I rolled my eyes to the flaking ceiling. "And what we gon' do with fifty dollars? I need some clothes. I don't have nothin'! Nothin'! All my stuff was upstairs and the crackheads stole it."

"You need to take a chill pill. Stop sweatin' er'thing. So what, we only got fifty dollars. It's fifty dollars more than what we had. And no, it can't buy us no clothes, but it can get us some Chinese and at least we got some bus fare."

I looked down at my faded black jeans and oversized white tee. "I can't wear this nowhere. I look stupid."

"You can wear it to the mall."

"To the mall for what?"

"So we can get us some clothes."

"And how we gon' do that?"

18

The bridge is over

"Word is bond," Yvette squealed, as we walked swiftly outta the mall and rushed to the nearest bus stop. "Everything we got is fresh to def," she whispered as we slung two overflowing duffel bags across our shoulders.

Truthfully, I was a little paranoid. 'Cause I'd never done anything like this before. I mean, robbing a drug dealer was one thing, but runnin' up in the mall and boostin' was low budget and honestly, not even worth bail money.

But I was willing to roll with it, 'cause we ain't have no clothes and no other way of gettin' some. So, we hustled our way through Lerner's and helped ourselves to summer wardrobes.

The bus pulled up and we stepped on, hurrying to the back. We stuffed our bags under our seat and sat down.

"We gon' be stupid fresh." Yvette giggled.

"Yup." I grinned. "And you know it. And the next time we come back we could steal enough to sell to our crew."

"True. 'Cause I know Munch gon' be sweatin' these pink leather shorts."

"Sell 'em to her. Make some money and then come back and getchu some more."

"Not. I'm rockin' these. Psst. Please."

"Look, like Face always said, 'The only thing that ain't gotta price is loyalty.' Which means that er'thing else gotta tag, including them pink leather shorts."

"Face didn't know everything. 'Cause if he did he wouldn't be locked up right now."

Did she just chop me in the throat? *Breathe.* "Yvette, why would you say somethin' ill like that?" I looked toward the front of the bus and watched the driver help an old lady to her seat.

"What's ill about it?"

"The way you said it. You ain't say all that when you used to be sweatin' him. For all I know, Face might be Kamari's daddy. 'Cause truth be told she looks like Queenie to me."

"You waaaay outta pocket. I know who my baby father is. And I wasn't never sweatin' Face."

"You lyin'? We was even planning a double wedding before."

"Not true."

"Yes, it is. And anyway, if it's not true, then what you mad for?"

"I ain't mad." She shrugged. "Who said I was mad? I'm just sayin' that I wasn't sweatin' him. I mean, maybe you was sweatin' K-Rock, but I ain't see Face like that."

"You can't be serious."

"Excuse me. You two."

Me and Yvette looked up and there was a uniformed officer staring down at us.

I sucked in a breath and hoped he couldn't hear my heart skipping beats. I looked down at the duffel bags we had poking from under the seat. Then I looked over at Yvette and she'd turned to stone.

"Get up!" the cop snapped and gripped me by my forearm, pinching his fingertips into my skin.

"Get offa me!" I screamed.

"You two are under arrest!" he said, as another officer reached for Yvette.

"For what?!" I snapped.

"For shoplifting."

"I ain't steal nothing!" I tried to snatch away but couldn't.

An officer handcuffed me and yanked me off of the bus and his partner dragged a handcuffed Yvette behind me.

The whole bus was buzzin'. Some kids was laughin' and others was in awe. Old ladies was shakin' they heads, complaining about how this didn't make any sense and we should be ashamed of ourselves. And everybody else was just watchin' and lookin' at us like this was an episode of *Miami Vice* unfolding right in front of them.

I couldn't believe this was really happening. The whole bus was filled with police. You woulda thought we was some real thieves. By the time the officers escorted us back into the mall and tossed us into the security room, Yvette had completely fallen apart. I was doing my best to hold it down for the both of us. All I kept praying is that this fool remembered not to talk. 'Cause as far as I was concerned, I didn't know whose stuff this was.

The security room was filled with television monitors that zoomed in on just about every angle in every store. There was a double mirror that showed the front door. There was also a table that held all of the stuff we'd stolen and two chairs, which we were handcuffed to.

"So you like to steal," an officer said to us. His eyes going from me to Yvette and back again. "A buncha thieves!"

"I need to call my grandmother," I spat.

The officer snorted. "We don't have to let you make a call. We could send you straight to juvie and call child welfare."

"Whatever."

"Oh, you're a little smart aleck, huh?"

I didn't even respond to that. "You arresting us or what?" I snapped. "Otherwise I need to call my grandmother to come and get me."

The door opened and the manager from the store we licked off stepped into the room. "Yes! These two! That's them, right there!" She shook her head. "I can't believe this! They are no older than my daughter and are out here stealing! You need to be worried about school! Not ripping people off! I feel sorry for your parents!"

"Trick," I spat. "I don't need you to feel sorry for me! I got this. Who you should feel sorry for is your mother 'cause she gave birth to a beast."

"Ma'am," an officer interrupted, "I'd like to step into another room to discuss the charges with you."

"I need to call my grandmother!" I yelled.

One of the officers frowned as he spat. "What's the number?"

"555-1212," I said. The officer dialed the number and held the phone to my ear.

Nana picked up on the first ring. "Praise the Lord. God is good."

"Nana, it's Isis."

"What is it?" I could hear her taking a pull of her cigarette.

"Me and Yvette need your help."

"My help?" She blew out the smoke.

"They got us up here in Livingston Mall. Claiming we

were stealing, when we were not. They got stuff up here on the table and I don't know who this mess belongs to. And I don't know where they got the idea that it belongs to us."

Nana snorted. "I don't think that's a bad idea, actually. 'Cause you two didn't have no money to even cross the street, but you up there at the mall. And you at the mall the same day that Bill said fifty dollars was missing from his wallet. I think I'm beginning to put two and two together."

"Nana—"

"And Yvette left this dang-gon' baby here and ain't said nothin' to nobody. Just walked out the door? I gotta good mind to leave both y'all lil thievin' asses right where you at and call the state for this lil brat. I don't want no kids. I done raised mine. And I'm not gon' raise no baby. And you two lil thievin' whores. Didn't I tell you I didn't like thieves? I just told you this."

"I'm not no thief!"

"Shut up! 'Cause you ain't nothing. And you ain't gon' never be nothin' 'cause yo' mama's a slut monkey and daddy is some garbage. Betchu can't call him to come for you. 'Cause he's just like his daddy. Garbage."

"You comin' or what?"

"I got a good mind to leave you there, let 'em take you to jail, and have the dykes make men outta you."

"Nana—"

"Don't Nana me. My name is Darleen. Now mark this, if I decide to ask Bill to bring me up there to get you two, this will be the last time I come and get you. So if your stealing behinds get the urge to go five-finger discount shopping again, don't even dial my number. Lose it."

Click.

The officer hung up the phone and shook his head.

Two hours passed and I started to think maybe Nana wasn't coming. I knew for sure we were about to be carted out of here and taken downtown. I could tell by how bad Yvette was crying that she was thinking the same thing.

But then: "Jesus is the truth and the light." There was Nana standing there. I'd never been so happy to see her.

"Nana!" I said, and me and Yvette smiled.

"Yes, ma'am," Nana said to the female officer standing next to her. "That's them." She held a sleeping Kamari on her shoulder. "And I'm so, so sorry." She looked at the store manager. "Apologize." She looked over at us, arching a brow. "Now."

I started to say, "For what?" But changed my mind. "We're sorry."

"And that you are," Nana said. She turned to the store manager. "I know that their fate lies in your hands and I'm not here to persuade you of anything. I just want you to know that they were not raised to be thieves. But when your mothers are junkie whores and you don't know your fathers, there's only so much a grandmother can do."

The store manager grabbed Nana's hand. "I'm sure you are doing the best you can."

"I am." Nana sniffed. "I am. And they are good girls. They are."

"They don't need to be stealing."

"You're right. They don't. And if there's any way I can pay you back for the stuff they took, then please tell me what I owe you. I'm on a fixed income, but praise God, anything is possible."

The manager shook her head. "I should really, really

press charges on you girls. Your grandmother is doing the best she can and this is the thanks she gets. Ma'am." She turned to Nana. "Looks like I have back everything they took. So I'm willing to forget this whole incident, as long as I don't see their faces in my store again."

"Hallelujah!" Nana waved her hand to Jesus. She looked at us and said, "Say thank you!"

"Thank you," we mumbled. The officers uncuffed us and Nana handed Kamari to Yvette.

"Truly appreciate this ma'am," Nana said. "And don't worry, you won't have to see their faces again."

I fought with everything in me not to cuss the whole room out, and especially Nana 'cause this chick was off the meat rack. But since I didn't wanna push my luck, I stayed quiet.

Mr. Bill was asleep by the time we made it to the car. But he hopped up when we got in and slammed the door.

"Everything all right?" He snorted, wiping the cold from his eyes.

"Yeah, it's cool," Nana said, turning around toward the back seat. "These two lil bird-brain bimbos wanna steal their way through life, moving around here like thieves in the night. Now I got to tie down and lock up everything I own, 'cause now that Stick has been tossed out into the street, she's been replaced by two more thieves. Goons. Now I don't know where you gon' get the money from and I don't care. All I know is that you better get it from somewhere 'cause Bill need his gas back and I need some money for misconvenience."

"It's inconvenience," I mumbled, looking out the window and sinking down into my seat.

I swear this was not my life.

My life had my fly daddy, dressed in his smooth and loud-color suits. Queenie sittin' in the kitchen baggin' up pounds of weed. Face plottin' and schemin'. Schooly dreamin'. Yvette gigglin'. Break dancin'. And B-boys. And hip-hop. And stupid-fresh kicks. And a dope radio blastin' my mix-tapes in the window.

I needed somebody—somewhere—to tell me what happened to my yesterday. Why did Queenie just jet and leave me here? Was my posters still in my room? Was my weed still tucked away in my nightstand drawer? Was mothersuckers down at the playground still scared of me? Was I still thorough? Down by law?

Or was I this weak and pathetic nothin' stuck here, with a beautiful life that had withered to dog shit.

19

Jungle love

Three years later: 1989

"**B**aby Girl! Look atchu! All grown up and lookin' just like yo' mama! And you finally made it to see yo' daddy."

I couldn't believe he said that.

I blinked. Then looked away.

I couldn't look at him.

I just couldn't.

So, I looked around Ms. Brenda's apartment, my eyes skipping from the torn plastic that covered the floral living room set, to the moving boxes stacked along the walls, to Yvette—who stood next to me.

I pulled in and pushed out a deep breath, then looked back over to Daddy. He was dressed in a worn pair of blue jeans, an oversized plaid shirt, and construction boots, and he held a half-empty Olde English forty in his hand.

Most of me was happy to see him and the rest of me was scared that he wouldn't remember who I was.

Although he still lived in Da Bricks, I hadn't really seen him in the last three years. But since today was my sixteenth birthday I decided to do something different and knock on Ms. Brenda's door.

"Who's that, Daddy?" A little girl stood in front of Daddy and leaned against his legs.

"That's your sister Isis." He sipped his beer. "She just stopped by for a moment to say hello."

I felt like I'd been kicked in the gut and I didn't know whether it was this lil girl calling my daddy, Daddy, or him limiting the time I wanted to spend with him to a moment.

The little girl continued, "Oh." She smiled. "My name is Jacinda. You goin' wit' us? 'Cause we movin' to Baltimore."

Before I could answer or even wrap my mind around what Jacinda had just said to me, Daddy shook his head and said, "No, baby. Isis is a big girl now. She's not going to live with us. Just me, you, Mommy, and your other sisters and brothers."

"Okay." The little girl hunched her shoulders, gave me a small wave, and ran off.

And that's when it hit me. . . . He'd lied to me.

He lied.

Set me up.

Made me believe I was a princess.

When I wasn't.

Made me believe he would always be here for me.

When he wasn't.

I felt like I could barely stand up and if I didn't sit down, I was gon' fall. So I flopped down on the plastic-covered sofa, next to the door.

Daddy grinned. "Talk to me. Tell me how's er'body at the house? How's your grandmother?"

Fat. Always mad. Hates everybody, except her boyfriend. "She's fine. Likes to keep the house clean." I swallowed and wiped the tears I felt crawling to the corners of my eyes. I even tossed in a small smile.

"That's mama." He looked over at Yvette. "And how you been?"

"Okay." Yvette sucked her teeth, draping an arm over my shoulders.

"Isis," Daddy said. "How's Chuck, and what's going on with Stick?"

Chuck's on the run. Streets said he killed a dude. I hate Stick. She has stole, sold, and smoked up er'thing I had. And I didn't have nothin' to begin with. "They fine."

"How's Face?"

"In prison."

Daddy shook his head.

Tears eased out the corners of my eyes. I sniffed and quickly wiped them away.

Daddy paused and took in my tears. "Smile, baby girl, your daddy's okay."

Your daddy's okay? Did he just say...your daddy's okay?

He really thought my tears was about him? I promise you, I wanted to punch him in his face.

Was he trippin'?

Crazy?

He had to be.

'Cause ain't no way he was serious.

I did all I could to fight it, but I couldn't hold it in any more. Bump this. "First of all, I'm not cryin' over you!"

"Then tell me what's wrong."

"Er'thing is wrong! What part you got messed up? You so busy askin' about er'body else that you ain't asked about me yet? You wanna know how I'm doin'?!" I pounded the arm of the couch, wishing it was his face. "Huh? What about me? Don't you wanna know how I'm doin'?" Before he could answer, I blew up the spot. "Yo' fat mama don't give a right tittie-freak about me. Just don't mess wit Jesus, her money, her man, or her cigarettes and she'll let you live in peace. But that's all she gon' do!" Hot tears continued to pour down my face but I flung them away.

"Queenie? Don't nobody know where she's at. You over here playin' a ghetto Mike Brady and you think, you really, really think, my tears is about whether you okay or not? I just turned sixteen today, don't you think I need somebody to take care of me!"

"I did the best I could—"

"You ain't do nothing!"

"Your mother put me out!"

"She should've put you out!" I hopped up from my seat. "I hate I even came here. Forget you! I don't need you! I'm good and I can take care of myself."

"You outta order, baby girl!"

"I'm not outta order! You outta order! You and Queenie. Got me out here by myself. Livin' wit' people who don't like me. Keep stealin' from me! Did you even realize that today is my birthday?! Do you understand I don't have nothin'?! Face locked up. At least he got three hots and a cot. But me? Zero. Zilch. Nada. Nothin'. Not even you!" I kicked a stack of his boxes and they tumbled down and scattered across the floor.

A pregnant Ms. Brenda stormed from the back of the apartment and into the living room. She looked over at Daddy. "Zeke, if she don't quiet down and sit down you gon' have to get her up and out of here!"

"Forget you!" I snapped. "This is between me and my father. You need to mind your business!"

"This is my business."

"You don't have no business between them!" Yvette snapped. "So take yo' fat self back where you came from and go have a seat."

"Zeke!" Ms. Brenda spat. "You gon' let them talk to me like that? They gotta go! Right now!"

I could tell that Daddy felt bad. But so what? I'm glad he felt like that 'cause he needed to feel what I'd been feeling for the last three years. Like nothing.

"Don't even sweat it, Daddy. I understand perfectly." I looked over at Yvette. "You ready?"

"Yup."

"Let's go." We stormed out and as the door slammed behind us, I heard Ms. Brenda tell Daddy that we better not ever come back.

20

Salley from the valley

"Surprise and happy birthday, hookerrrrrrrrrrrr!" Munch screamed the moment me and Yvette stepped into our bedroom.

I struggled to smile and forget about the fight I'd just had with Daddy, as Yvette, Munch, and Cali snatched me into a group hug and we all danced around.

"This heifer is finally sixteen with us!" Cali screamed. "And we gon' do it up today, baby! What y'all wanna do?"

"Well, first she gon' open these gifts. And then we gon' hit this blunt." Yvette smacked her lips in glee. She pointed to her bed, which was filled with gifts, and over to my nightstand, which held a freshly rolled blunt. She pushed me over toward her bed.

"This heifer's been boosting again." I chuckled and hugged Yvette, who had never given up and had perfected the art of lickin' off the mall. Me? I learned my lesson. I liked to look fly, but I wasn't about to go to jail behind no jeans, so while my cousin was out five-finger shopping, I kept her baby.

"That is not all from boosting." Yvette smiled. "Flip gave me some money and some of those things I actually had to buy."

Me, Cali, and Munch all looked at each other, our eyes bright with surprise. "So you claimin' his old behind now?" I smirked but then quickly smiled, to not spoil the mood.

"Funny," she said. "Don't even try it. You knew he was Kamari's daddy all along. I just never said anything because I didn't want him to go to jail."

"'Cause you know Nana woulda had him locked down."

"I know."

"So y'all still a couple?"

She sucked her teeth. "Please. He done had like three or four babies since Kamari. So I left him alone."

"Good," Munch said. "Now let's get back to the party." She snapped her fingers. "Open the gifts."

I flopped down in the middle of Yvette's bed and tore into gift boxes filled with Levi's jeans, mini skirts, tops, and sneakers. "Oh my God! This stuff is so fly."

"I know it is," Yvette said proudly, handing me a small red velvet box.

"That's from all of us," Cali said.

"What is it?" I said, as I opened it. There was a gold chain inside with a small charm that was round on one end and L-shaped on the other.

"We each have one too!" Munch said and they all lifted their gold chains. "And if you put all the charms together it makes a heart."

"This is soooooooo dope!" I screamed.

"We know," Cali said. "And now we got something that represents our crew."

"We sure do!" I said as they all fell across Yvette's bed and we group hugged again. "Now," I said, wiping tears of joy from my face. "Let's hit this blunt."

For the next hour, we zooted up, talked about boys, clothes, and rappers we'd love to do. "I think LL Cool J is everything and more," Cali said. "I would love to rock out with him."

"I bet you would," I said. "Isn't that who James told you he looked like?"

"Eww." She wrinkled her nose. "I broke up with him."

"You did?" Munch said. "I'm your sister and you didn't even tell me that."

"We just broke up last night."

I couldn't help but laugh. "How you break up with somebody you've never seen? I mean, you met him on the party line. If you wanted to leave him alone, all you had to do was stop calling."

We all cracked up, including Cali. "I'm not worried. I'll find me another boo."

"Me too," Yvette said.

"Me three," I agreed.

"Well, I'm happy. My baby loves me," Munch said.

"Whatever." We laughed.

Munch asked, "Hey, y'all know where I haven't been in mad years?"

"Where?" they asked simultaneously.

"To the park to chill."

"I know," Yvette agreed. "'Cause all we do is hang around here."

Cali jumped in, "That's 'cause we stay broke as a joke."

"Word," Munch added.

"But I got some money today." Yvette grinned. "And if I hit Nana off with twenty dollars, she'll keep Kamari for me. So y'all wanna go? I got our bus fare."

We all hopped off the bed so fast, it's a wonder we didn't take off and fly. "Let's get it!" I popped my hips to the left and then to the right. I was having one of the best days of my life, and I refused to let the emptiness of not having Daddy, Queenie, Face, or Schooly here with me sink in. I had my girls and right now, at this moment, that was all that mattered to me and all the family I needed.

21

Lookout weekend

The moment we stepped into the playground, I felt like everything had been on pause and waitin' for me. The trees. The breeze. The birds. The swelterin' summer sun that beamed down at least eighty-five degrees. And the deejay, who rocked the dopest hip-hop, courtesy of his turntable and two massive and boomin' speakers connected to yards of extension cord that snaked from somebody's apartment window and eased down the block.

Er'thing was live and the park was clearly the place to be.

I looked dope too: white and neon-paint-splattered midriff tee that draped off one shoulder. Super tight and white Levi jeans. Crisp white Lottos on my feet with fat hot-pink shoestrings. All courtesy of the Get Fresh Clique.

Me and Yvette grooved to the music, while Munch and Cali flirted with cuties.

People was everywhere.

B-boys was break dancing.

D-boys was shootin' dice.

The think-they-dime girls were posted up.

The chill chicks were sprinkled here and there.

And kids were all over the monkey bars, the seesaws, and the swings.

"Isis," poured from behind me. "So what? Don't tell me you gon' try and pretend like you don't remember me."

I found myself holding my breath and forcing my mouth to fight off a smile. I could tell by the look in Yvette's eyes that that voice belonged to K-Rock. I turned around and couldn't fight off my grin a moment longer. "Oh my God! Wassup? How you been? Where you been?" I said practically in the same breath. "What's good?!"

"You. That's what's good." His caramel eyes drank me in. "Daaaaaang, girl. Look at lil Icy. All grown up for real. How old are you now?"

"Sixteen." *Jesus, I was blushing. Why, oh why, was I blushing? I needed to stop. Jesus, please help me to stop!* "Today's my birthday, actually."

"Word? Happy birthday, lil ma."

Lil ma? Lil ma? I felt like bustin' out into a moonwalk. I can't believe he didn't call me lil sis. "Thank you."

"So what do you have planned?" he asked.

Being here is the plan. Oh wait, I can't say that. Then I'ma sound all played, busted, and disgusted. Think... think... think... "I'ma chill with my man. He should be here at any moment." I popped my glossy lips and looked him dead in the eyes. Dang, he was fine.

"That's wassup."

"Yup. So what you got goin' on? Where have you been?"

"Yo, after Schooly died and they knocked my boy Face, I knew I had to switch it up or I was next."

"So what you do different?"

"I stopped slangin', got back in school like I needed to, and now I'm in college."

"College? Word up? Get outta here."

"Yeah, I'm only home for the summer."

"Where you school at?"

"Stiles U in New Orleans."

"That's wassup." I paused and a moment of awkward silence slipped in between us. I felt like he was checkin' for me, but I wasn't sure and I dang-gon' was not about to play myself. "Okay, well. I just saw my boo come into the park. I'll see you around."

He nodded, looked me up and down. "Okay. You got a man, huh?"

I forced a smile on my face. "Yup."

He nodded. "A'ight, I hope he treating you good. Doing you all right and holding you down."

"He is."

"Straight. That's wassup. So I'ma let you go. I'm not gon' hold you. Be good, lil ma."

"I will."

He gave me a soft kiss on the forehead before walking off and disappearing into the distance.

It took everything in me, or out of me, not to pass out. "Did you see him?" I squealed, as I turned around and faced Yvette. "He was sooooooo fly."

"He was all right," Yvette said. "But let me show you somebody soooooo fly that he has got to be illegal. I promise you the letters in his version of fly stand for fine, lovely, and yes, he is all of that."

"Who are you talkin' about?" I spun around and faced the B-boys, who were havin' a break-dancin' war. "Them?" I frowned. "I'm all for break dancin' but umm...dear Yvette, you already know you cannot come up offa nobody in a Windbreaker suit. I'm talkin' no cash, and a broke dude is just all kinds of wrong."

"Eww. Don't play me out like that." She curled her top lip. "My need-to-be tender is over there at three o'clock." She placed her hands on both of my shoulders and turned me to the left. I now faced the D-boys playin' a dice game. I pulled a long and soothing breath of fresh air into my nose and eased it through my glossy lips. "Daaaaang, they smell like money."

"Oh yes, they do." Yvette drooled.

"And judging by the groupies surrounding them, er'body wanna go to the bank." I snapped my fingers and my eyes soaked in the small dope boy crowd of Bermuda Kangols, Yankee caps, Levi's denim suits, and Adidas sweat suits. "Yvette, which check you tryna cash?"

"The honey-colored one with the sun shining over him. You see him?"

"The one in the dark blue Levi's suit?"

"Yes."

"He is lookin' stupid fresh."

"And did you peep the two dookie chains hanging around his neck? I just love him." She squealed and it was obvious that the butterflies in her belly were dancing. "They call him Fresh."

"Oh, word. How you know him?"

"Everybody know him."

"I don't."

"Umm, helloooo." She snapped her fingers. "Fresh is the head of the Avenues *and* er'body knows that the Avenues practically got hustlin' in the South Ward on lock."

"So he a Down South boy?" I took a step back. "You already know I hate Down South dudes!"

"Look. Most of them dudes that was out there when Schooly got killed and Face was in the game is either dead or in jail. I mean, it's still some on the block, but Fresh is not one of 'em. He's just cool wit' 'em. But he ain't a part of they crew."

"How you know that?"

"'Cause I know. Trust me, he's a cool dude."

"If you say so."

"I say so," she assured me. "And if I get wit' him, that's gon' be like gettin' wit' the president." She placed her right hand like a visor over her eyes. "The haters gon' be like, 'I see you, Yvette.'"

I laughed. "You really on his sack right now."

"Not yet, but I will be." She fanned her face. "How do I look?"

I looked her over in her black bodysuit, leopard leggings, and pumps. "Fresh."

"Fresh? Or stupid fresh?"

"Fresh enough to be Mrs. Fresh."

She giggled. "You sure?"

"Yes."

"Cool. Now how should I get his attention? 'Cause he has not looked my way." We both zoomed in on him. He was pickin' up the pot of money from the dice game he'd obviously won. He looked over at his boys, said something to them, and lay a hundred-dollar bill on the ground.

I pulled a cherry-red Blow Pop from my pocket, threw the wrapper on the ground, and placed the candy between my lips. After a few seconds of the sweetness drenching my tongue, I wiggled my neck and said, "Don't be shy. Walk over there and say, 'Heyyyyyyyy, Fresh. Wassup, playboy. What's good, young blood?'"

She shoved her hands up on her hips. "I'm serious."

"Me too."

"Isis, you knoooow I'm not gon' do that."

"Okay, okay, I got an idea. Come on." I took a step toward Fresh and his crew.

Yvette pulled me back. "No wait. We can't go over there! He's gon' think I'm desperate. He needs to come to me."

"What?" I shook my head and looked at her like she was crazy. I couldn't believe this. This skeezer had stolen er'thing that wasn't nailed down, but now she was too scared to step to a dude? I frowned. "You want him?"

"Yeah."

"You tryna come up?"

"Yeah."

"Then you better get your rap together. Queenie always said if the john don't come to the track, then you go to where they at and make a new track. Maybe he see you. Maybe he don't. But if you for sure wanna be seen, then I'ma make sure he lays eyes on you. Now do have a hundred dollars?"

"What?" She looked at me like I had two heads. "Oh heck no! What you need a hundred dollars for?"

"So you have it?"

"Yeah, but I need that for my baby. That's all I got and Kamari needs Pampers, milk, and food."

"Gimme the money."

"I can't do that."

"Would you give it to me?!"

"No!"

"You'll get it back today. I promise."

Yvette hesitated, then reluctantly handed me the money. "That's all the money I got left for the month."

"Look, go sit over there on the bleachers, post up, and look cute. I got a plan, just follow my lead."

"And what's your plan?"

"I'ma hook you up. Now go," I said, tight-lipped.

"No! Suppose he has a girlfriend?"

"Suppose he doesn't?"

"Don't make me look desperate."

"Go sit down."

Yvette huffed, but she walked over to the bleachers and took a seat.

I walked over to the dope boys and winked, then I slowly bent down and lay my money on top of theirs. I stood back up and gave each of them a wide grin. I could hear Yvette clearing her throat, but I refused to turn around. I already knew I was takin' a chance and I didn't need her making me nervous. Besides, if things went the way I planned, I was gon' walk away with a pot of cash and Yvette was gon' have her man.

Fresh and his entire crew turned and had their eyes on me. Obviously, nobody had ever jumped into their dice games before. I took my lollipop out of my mouth and looked at Fresh. "What? You don't play with girls?"

He shook his wrist and the herringbone bracelets he wore draped over his hand. "Money is money. And girl or no girl, if you wanna lose yours to me and my crew, then you're welcome to. So come on, sexy, and get your money taken away."

"Oh, that was real cute. And whatchu call that? Reverse psychology, tryna make think I'ma lose. Well, I don't lose and I'll have you to know that I prevail in er'thing I do."

Fresh's crew gave amused sighs and some of them outright laughed. "Say word?" Fresh said more to his crew than to me.

"Word," I said.

"So you think you just gon' not only invite yo'self into

our game but you gon' take our money too?" He laughed, and for a moment there, I thought I saw a blush.

"First time for everything."

Fresh stroked his box beard and judging by the redness filling his cheeks, he was fighting off a smile. "So who you s'pose to be? A hood celebrity?"

"Maybe. And could you come on, 'cause you're talking a little too much. Now gimme the dice. Ladies roll first." I looked over my shoulder at Yvette and winked.

I could tell by the dreamy look on her face that the butterflies in her stomach were fluttering all over the place, again.

"Who is that?" Fresh asked.

"Your new girl. My cousin Yvette."

"My new what?" He chuckled.

"Unless you already have a girl, then you should probably break up with her tonight. So let's roll the dice and when you take my cousin on a date, then the two of you can work out the kinks and the details."

"So a hundred dollars and a date with your cousin is what you tossin' into the pot?"

"Yop."

"And what if I win, then what I'ma get out the game?"

"Well, for one, if you win, or any of your other boys win—"

"They ain't in this round." He placed three hundred-dollar bills on the ground, lifted my money off the original pot, and placed it on top of his.

I arched a brow. "Well, if you win, then you get the whole pot."

"And?"

"*And*, you get a chance to go out on a date with my cousin, Yvette."

"And why should I do that?"

" 'Cause she's cute *and* she's feelin' you."

"Look around. They all feelin' me." He looked back over his shoulder at Yvette, and then quickly turned back around to me. "A'ight, bet but—"

"No buts." I picked up the dice and shook them in my hand. "Now blow on these 'cause mama needs some shoes and my cousin needs to be rockin' witchu." I squatted, prepared to roll the dice.

Fresh squatted beside me and placed his hand over mine. "Hold up. I didn't finish."

"Finish."

"If you win, I'ma take your cousin out. But if I win"—he lifted his hand and blew on the dice—"I wanna date with you."

22

Nothin' but a faker

"You know I ain't goin', right?" Yvette sat on the edge of her bed, while Kamari sat between her legs and Yvette braided her hair. She parted Kamari's hair and slid a fingertip full of Dax grease onto her scalp.

"You buggin'." I sat Indian style in the middle of my bed. "I won the game. So Fresh has a date with you tonight. But you wanna send me? How whack is that? I already told you I would babysit. Why you sweatin' it?"

"This isn't about you babysittin'." She frowned. "This is about me not going out with a dude who's really feelin' you. I ain't desperate and I am def not on him like that. You didn't make him think that, did you?"

"Heck no. You know better than that. I don't think you're desperate and neither does he." I turned over and leaned forward, propped on both elbows. "But believe me, he really wants to go out with you. After I won the game, he said, 'Tell your cousin to be ready at seven o'clock.'"

Yvette picked up her pink beeper and looked at the

time. "Then you better hurry up and shower. It's six-thirty."

"Yvette."

"Isis, I'm not going."

"Well, I'm not going either. Bump that."

"Chick, please. Fresh is a cute D-boy wit' some dough. And you need to top your birthday off by spending it with him."

"I had a dope birthday spending it with my crew."

"Yeah, well, spending time with your crew is one thing, but spending time with the illest player around is another thing. Unless, of course you secretly over there waitin' on K-Rock to slide through." She paused, and cocked her neck to the side. "We both know he's your real crush groove."

"Slow down, low down. Relax. K-Rock is a'ight. But that's it. He ain't slangin' no more, so around here that means he's—"

"Broke as joke."

"Exactly. He done fell off and turned into some college boy. What I look like to you—?"

"Like you might be hung up on Mr. College."

I just stared at Yvette long and hard, 'cause it seemed she forgot that I was the cousin who would kick her right in the throat for talking slick. I mean...I was checkin' for K-Rock, a little bit. He was cute and all, but that's as far as it went. "Yvette, don't make me bring out the almighty Isis on you."

She fell out laughing. "Look, you can sit over there and fantasize about Ke'Ron 'K-Rock' 'College Boy' Green or you can drop the thoughts about that zero and get wit' a hero. And anyway, do you know how being seen on Fresh's arm is gon' elevate your birthday to stupid dumb dope? Word up, you straight played out if you don't go."

"So you want me to be a faker? A sucker? A gold digger. Knowin' I don't like this dude but going out with him just 'cause he's a baller?"

Yvette looked at me like I had lost my mind. "Why you lyin'? You was cheesin' just as hard as he was. And that's cool. It ain't like you doin' me dirty or anything. I keep tellin' you that it's no sweat. So stop tryna act like you not feelin' him. 'Cause you are."

"You buggin' and besides, it's a million boys out there and I don't need to chill with that one. I'll pass."

Yvette popped her lips. "That's on you. But ain't no need to front for me, 'cause from where I'm sittin', we in the same boat and don't neither one of us have nothin'. And what little we do have, I stole."

"What does that have to do with anything? Or are you sayin' again that I should use him?"

"I'm sayin' you need to have fun and hit the streets. Stop worrying about me, 'cause I'ma do me. All day. Now if you don't wanna go, then don't. But personally, I'ma think you stupid for staying here."

"Stupid?"

"Real dumb. Here you got a moneymaker tryna kick it to you and you frontin' like a church whore."

I hesitated, a part of me was kind of ticked that Yvette was coming at me all crazy, but she was right. I was feelin' Fresh. "You sure you wouldn't care? It really wouldn't matter?"

"Umm, no. That's what I keep sayin' to you. Now getcho butt up and go get fly."

I hopped up from my bed and slapped my feet on the floor. "I don't even know what to wear."

"That neon-pink and black striped mini dress with the fishnet gloves I got you."

My eyes grew bright with excitement. "That dress is sooooo ill."

"Of course it is. I picked it out." She snapped her fingers. "Now hurry up and go shower so I can do your hair and makeup."

23

Lover girl

"And just where *the hell* is yo' lil fresh behind goin'?" Nana snapped the moment I stepped into the living room and strutted past her and toward the front door. "Yo' fast tail ain't asked me for permission to go nowhere." She stood up from her recliner and slid her Keds, with the broken-down heel, onto her feet.

Psst. Please. I ain't never asked you for permission to do nothin', not even live here. I rolled my eyes to the ceiling and it crossed my mind that I didn't really owe this musty tramp an explanation. And technically, I could ignore her bearilla behind. But I didn't. "I'm goin' out." I turned and faced her.

"Out where, heifer?" she asked, with her mouth twisted.

"Out. Side."

"Out. Side. Where, streetwalker?"

"Out. Side. The. Door."

She shoved a hand up on her hip and tapped a foot.

I placed my hand on the knob and twisted it.

She continued, "So you just gon' walk up outta here anyway. You don't give a rat's behind what I say."

Silence.

"This is exactly why I can't stand y'all asses. I curse the day yo' whorin' mama and drunk daddy ran off without you. And I'll be glad when they come back to get you and whoever Yvette's parents really is come and collect her too. And don't think I don't know she out there hustlin' and stealin' clothes!" she yelled loud enough for the whole house to hear. "And my guess is, wit' that stolen dress crawled up yo' butt, that you takin' up yo' mama and daddy ho business. I tell you what though, don't come back in here wit' no HIV and no secret babies. 'Cause the next retarded mothersucker that crosses that door will be donated to the state and you can believe that."

"Is that it?"

"What the...?" Nana rushed over toward me and stepped two feet into my personal space. "What do you mean, is that it? Is what it?"

I sighed. I shoulda just left, now this trick is blocking the door. "Is that it?" I arched a brow. "Are you finished? I've heard this *allllll* before. 'Cause you keep saying it. I don't need to hear it again. So yeah, is that it? Are you done or are you gon' add your famous line about how you shoulda put a foot up our behinds a long time ago? Or you gon' save that for when I come back?"

"See, yo' frickin' attitude is the very reason why you ain't gon' be no more than that whore and that wino who made you. Matter of fact, you might be less than that. Gon' stand up in my face, like you grown as me. I don't care if it's your birthday. All I care about is how soon you gon' be eighteen so you can get up and outta here. You up in here eatin' my food, runnin' my bills up, and you think you gon' talk grown to me—"

"You act like you don't get no money for us. Me and Yvette both on your welfare grant, and you not gon' put us out no time soon, 'cause then you won't get that money. So chill and back away from the door."

Nana squinted and for a moment I just knew she was about to slap me, but she didn't. "I don't care whatchu do." She sat back down in her chair. "Just be back in this house at a decent hour or the chain will be up and you will be sleepin' out there in the courtyard."

"Yeah, okay." I didn't even toss a look her way. I just twisted the knob and walked out. A few moments later, I stepped off the elevator and into the courtyard, where Fresh was leanin' against the passenger side of a kitted-up black Maxima. The car was just as fly as he was. Windows tinted. System bumpin'. Rims shinin'.

Fresh wore a plum-colored linen dress shirt, tucked into a pair of dark gray and black two-tone jeans, showcasing his black MCM belt. A thick herringbone chain hung around his collar, and black shades shielded his eyes.

Dang, he is ill.

Fine.

Fly.

Stupid fresh.

He is so fresh I see why they call him Fresh.

Chill. Dudes can smell when you sweatin' 'em.

So relax.

Suck your stomach in.

Chew on the gum in your mouth extra hard to make sure your breath is straight, but try not to suck all the mint out.

You got this.

"Surprise." I stood before him and smiled.

Fresh lifted his shades, covered his mouth, and laughed.

"What's funny?" I popped my lips and put on a fake attitude, anything to keep from smiling.

"Nothing's funny." He softly flicked my chin.

"Then why are you laughin'?"

"'Cause...you got game, you know that? What happened to your cousin?"

"What? You want me to go and get her?" I pointed over my shoulder to Da Bricks. "'Cause I can."

"Chill, boo. You know I don't want that. No disrespect. She's cute and all, but I'm diggin' you. I just showed up to keep my word. The most Yvonne would've gotten outta me—"

"It's Yvette."

"Okay. Well the most Yvette would've gotten outta me was a trip to Burger King. I woulda let her get a large fry and a shake, and then dropped her off."

"Daaaaaang, it's like that? You wouldn't even get my cousin a whopper?"

"A'ight. And a whopper. Then I would've come back tomorrow to see what was up witchu."

I laughed. "And I would've sent you home too. Me and my cousin don't share boos. Once she went out with you, that would've been a wrap."

"Word? So I guess it's a good thing you switched places with her tonight then."

"Maybe. Maybe not. 'Cause if your idea of a fly date is Burger King, then maybe I need to rethink some things. After all, it is my birthday. Can I get a steak at least? Dang."

He boldly placed his hands on my hips. "If you stick

with me, you can get anything you want. So come on and tell me where you've always wanted to go." He opened the car's passenger-side door and I slid in.

I did all I could not to smile, but I couldn't fight it a moment longer, so as he draped one arm over my seat and drove off with the other, I let my smile blossom and let Da Bricks disappear behind me.

24

Cold chillin'

"How's your steak, baby?"

"It tastes just like cotton candy." I giggled as I leaned over and let my head fall into the crook of Fresh's neck, his cologne filling my nose. We were in New York City, at the circus. The freakin' circus and I couldn't believe it! When Fresh asked me to tell him someplace I'd always wanted to go, I knew I couldn't say to find Queenie, so I said, "The circus."

"The circus?" He blinked, as if he expected me to say anything but that. "You've never been to the circus?"

"Nope. Unless you count what goes on in Da Bricks. Other than that I have never been."

He smiled, nodded, and took off for the highway. "No sweat. You ain't said nothin' but a word."

"I hope you're having a good time," Fresh said, intertwining his fingers with mine, as the ringmaster performed hoop tricks with the lions. "'Cause this is all for you."

"I'm having a great time." I squealed, now watching the lions lie down and roll over. "Chilling here with you is like...straight illmatic. The illest matic. The ultimate."

"Illmatic? Chillin' with me is like illmatic?" Fresh stared, as if he couldn't believe that. "What? You a rapper?"

"Yop."

"So what they call you?"

"God the MC."

"Yeah, a'ight, that's Rakim."

"Okay, well then, I'm Goddess the MC." I paused. "What? You wanna hear me rhyme?"

"No."

I heard what he said, but I broke out into a freestyle anyway. I pointed my left hand like a gun and shook it. "Check it. One time for your mind. I left my wallet in El Segundo and I left my pick inside my afro."

"Ohhhhhh, hold up. Look atchu. Wait a minute, let me drop some beats in it." He cupped his hands on the sides of his mouth and popped the dopest human beatbox I'd ever heard before. I think he even had Doug E. Fresh beat.

I jumped up and out of my seat in excitement. "Yooooo, you did that! Oh my God! I'ma start calling you Hip-Hop." I did the Pac-Man dance.

"Shhhhhhh!" The woman in front of us turned completely around and looked at us like she was seconds from calling security.

"You shhhhh!" I swerved my neck. "You don't shhhh me. I not one of them funny-lookin' kids you got sittin' there. Now turn back around."

Fresh laughed. "My bad," he said to the lady and then looked at me and said, "No, baby, chill. You know we loud."

"And? So? That beatbox was hot though." I retook my seat.

"I know, right." He draped an arm over my shoulders. "But we need to watch the show."

Lions, tigers, bears, white horses, and elephants all performed stunts I never knew they could do. Girls swung from the ceiling, hanging by their hair. Unicycles were everywhere. A woman was sawed in half and then put back together. A man shoved a stick of fire down his throat. A midget flew out of a cannon, and before the show was over, twenty clowns climbed out of a Volkswagen.

By the time the ringmaster brought the show to a close, I just knew Fresh would be the perfect boyfriend. I didn't wanna seem desperate though, so I was not about to ask him when we could chill again. I was just gon' pray he told me. And sooooon!

"This has been the perfect night," I said, as we pulled up in front of Da Bricks.

"Yeah, this was decent," Fresh said, shifting his car in park. "I'm glad you enjoyed yourself, baby. 'Cause I definitely enjoyed you."

"For real?"

"Yeah." He flicked my chin. "I like you. A lot. And I can't wait for us to do this again."

Again! He said do this again! Chill. Calm down.

My heart skipped three beats and I was seconds from wiping invisible sweat off my face.

Breathe.

Breathe.

Now speak. "Awww. That is soooo sweet." I tried to contain my blush, but couldn't. I reached for his right hand and braided our fingers together. "I can't wait for us to do this again either. Just let me know when and I'll be waiting for you."

He smiled. "So, Isis. Tell me something."

"Whatchu wanna know?"

"Tell me what's up with you?"

"Whatchu mean?"

"What's good with you? Tell me what you're about."

Immediately my eyes sank into my lap. I'd never really thought about what I was about. What did that even mean? All I knew is that my yesterday was a world away from my today; and I had to deal with it. Period. "That's a interestin' question." I shrugged. "I never been asked that before.... I'm a good person. If that's what you're asking me. I got a good heart. But I'm thorough, I was raised to be down by law, and I ain't gon' let nobody cross me. Like that's not gon' go down. Not easily. I'm loyal and I can't wait for the day that I can get up and outta this rat trap."

"So what, you don't like where you live at?"

"Heck no. I used to love living here, but after my brother got killed, things changed. My family went their separate ways. And I've been staying with my grandmother ever since."

"Damn." He looked taken aback. "I'm real sorry to hear about your brother. What happened?"

A moment of awkward silence slipped in, then I changed the subject. "So now, Fresh, it's your turn. Tell me whatchu about."

Fresh looked into my eyes. "I'm the realest dude you ever gon' meet. I'm loyal. I run these streets. And I don't give my heart easily. I'ma always be here if you need me. Money is not an object, and as long as you belong to me, then I'ma give you the world. You think one day, after we get to know each other a little more, you could rock with that?"

I can rock with that right now. Today. At this moment.

Whaaaaaaat, we don't have to wait. Bump. That. Let's do this right now. "Yeah." I nodded. "After we get to know each other, I'm sure I could rock with that." I was tryin' hard not to grin from ear to ear. But it was such a freakin' struggle that it's a wonder I didn't break my jaw tryna hold my cheeks back. "You're pretty dope, you know that?" I slid my arms around his neck.

"Is that so?"

"Umm hmm." I bravely pressed my lips onto his. "Now it's one more thing I wanna know."

"What's that?"

"How dope are your kisses?"

"You tell me," he whispered against my lips, sliding his sweet tongue into my mouth and filling it with honey.

25

My buddy

Ms. Crabtree, I know that you're not mad at me 'cause I told you... blasted from some kid's boom box, as I walked out and into the courtyard. It had been a month since I'd hung out here. I'd been with Fresh day in and day out. Cold chillin' at his apartment. We shared blunts, popped champagne bottles just because, and even though I didn't have a license or a permit, he taught me how to drive his car.

There was even some nights, while he laid back and relaxed, watching TV, that he let me supervise the two naked chicks who cooked up his coke and turned it into crack.

And once I showed him that I knew how to properly weigh out and bag up ounces of weed, Fresh dismissed the chicks he had doing it and appointed me.

There was only one problem: Fresh hadn't made me his girl, yet. And I wasn't feelin' that. I needed a title and I deserved one. But since it seemed that he was comfortable with the definition of what we was s'pose to be dangling in the air, I knew I had to switch things up. So, this after-noon, when he woke up, the only thing he would find on the pillow next to him would be a freshly rolled blunt.

And that's it. 'Cause until he put a label on us, I was gon' take a step back, come home to Da Bricks, and chill wit' my clique.

"Where the heck have you been, heifer?" Cali said, as I walked over to the park bench where she sat.

I scooted next to her and kissed her on both of her rosy cheeks. "I missed you," I said, hugging her tightly.

"Yeah, right. Sure you did." She smiled and then twisted her lips. "School'll be starting back up in a minute and you haven't chilled with us since your birthday. You just forgot about your friends."

"No, I haven't. I just been spending some time with my baby."

"Yeah, I know. Yvette told me and Munch that you had a new man named Fresh you met in the park. She also said that ever since you started kickin' it with him, that you changed."

"Changed?"

"She said you was a whole other chick, straight feelin' yourself. And that it was almost like she ain't know you anymore."

I frowned. "A whole other chick? She don't know me anymore? Yvette said that? You sure?"

"Ask Munch. She was there. Yvette also said had she known that Fresh would stop you from bein' wit' us, she woulda never gave him to you. Did she really give him to you? How did that go down? Y'all sharing boyfriends now?"

"Umm, no, we're not. First of all, she didn't give him to me. She liked him, but he liked me. She told me to go out with him. But now she's taking that and stabbing me in the back wit' it? Word." I was pissed.

"She just misses you, that's all."

"Then she should've said, 'I miss my cousin.' Not all that other two-faced mess. I don't appreciate that. And second of all, y'all family and no dude could ever come between us. Period."

Cali hesitated. "Well…it did seem like you was no longer chillin' wit' us."

"I hate that you was thinking that."

"Me too. But anyway, I missed you."

"And I missed you."

"You better. 'Cause I got a bunch to tell you." Cali popped her lips.

"Like what?"

"Well, remember how Munch prided herself on being the virgin out the bunch?"

"Yeah." My eyes grew wide.

"Well, that cutie she met in the park, she let him bust her cherry in the backseat of some busted Pontiac."

"Say word."

"Word. And her period is late. If Cousin Shake find out she been gettin' busy, it's gon' be World War III up in that piece."

My mouth practically drooled. "I can't believe Munch gave up the goodies."

"Yup. And Yvette. I don't know wassup wit' her."

"Whatchu mean?"

"She back to messin' with that bum." Cali pointed across the street.

I looked up and we both watched as Flip speed-walked over to one of the corner boys and copped some dope. Then he continued walking up the block.

"And she know he dirty." I shook my head. "Yuck! I can't stand him. And I don't know why she hooked up with his old behind."

"Me either." Cali shook her head. "And she keep lying about it, but one day, I busted her."

"How?"

"'Cause I went up to y'all apartment looking for you, walked into y'all room, and they was tearin' them sheets up."

I couldn't believe this. I was gettin' sick to my stomach. "Don't tell me no more, Cali, 'cause you making me wanna throw up. I tell you what though, if he ever do anything to my cousin, I'ma slice his throat. And I put that on everything I love."

"For real though. Just call me before you slice, 'cause I bring guns to knife fights." She held her hand out and I slapped her five. "Now, let's get back to you and yo' boo. So y'all a couple now?"

I blushed. "Not yet, but soon…" I stopped mid-sentence and pointed at the dude crossing the street. "Cali, is that K-Rock?"

"Oh my God!" she said, waaaaay too excited. "I knew there was something else I meant to tell you. He was over here the other day shootin' hoops, and soon as me and Munch stepped outside, he stopped balling to ask us where you were. I think he feelin' you."

I squinted. "Why you say that?"

"'Cause the moment Munch said that you was with yo' man, he looked disappointed. But let me ask you this: since you got a man, can I chill wit' K-Rock?"

"No."

"But, according to Yvette, you all down for passing a man around and all I'm saying is pass him over here."

"No," I mumbled as K-Rock got closer.

"Is it because I'm white? You got something against the swirl? Is that why you doing this to me—"

"I forgot you was white. I thought you was Mexican."

"You lie."

"Would you stop being silly. And shhh, here he comes," I said, trying to wipe the blush off my face.

"Quick," Cali said. "Act like you don't see him."

"How?"

"Let's act like we asleep."

I looked at Cali like she was crazy and I couldn't help but to fall out laughing.

"Let me in on the joke," K-Rock said, the moment he stepped in front of me. "I wanna laugh too."

"It's nothing, really. What's up with you? What you doing here?"

"I came to shoot some hoops and then practice some boxing at the community center. I was checking for you the other day, but your homegirls told me you was out with ya man."

"I was."

"Oh." He nodded. "That's wassup. So how he treating you?"

"Good. Like I'm Isis the grown woman and not Icy the lil sis."

"So what does that mean? Y'all gettin' busy or somethin'?"

Oh nooooooo, he did not just nose-dive into my business like that. He must be tryna get popped dead up in the mouth. "Slow down. Do I ask you who you boom bustin' it wit'? Did I question you about that tree branch and whether or not you diggin' out her coochie?"

"Tree branch?"

"The chick you showed up wit' at Face's party."

"Face's party?" K-Rock squinted. "What party?"

"You knoooooow what party!" I swerved my neck.

"No, I don't. Face been locked up for three years. What party?" He paused. "Wait a minute. Hold up. Are you talking about Face's welcome home party?"

"Yop."

"Do you know how long ago that was?"

"And? Your point?"

"Why you sweatin' that? I don't even know where that chick is at."

"Whatever." I held back a grin. "I thought for sure y'all would've been married with two and a half kids and a St. Bernard by now."

"Umm." Cali smiled. I'd completely forgotten she was sittin' here. "What y'all really arguing about? Me and Cousin Shake was watchin' *Sally Jessy* the other day and this doctor said that when two people arguing, like this, that you need to dig deep and find out what the real issues are."

Me and K-Rock both looked at Cali like she had lost all control.

"It was a dope show though," she insisted.

"Catherine," I said, calling Cali by her government name. "You have lost your Mexican mind."

"Okay. Okay," she said, like she was throwin' the towel in. "I'ma let y'all breathe. Give you two a moment, only. 'Cause technically, I was sittin' here first. But I'ma go upstairs and see what's takin' my sister, Munch, so long to come down. Maybe her period came, or something. But hopefully, when I come back, you two would have worked things out, and I can have my seat back."

"Later, Cali," I said.

"Later, Isis. Later, K-Rock." She tossed a hand up behind her as she walked away and into the building she lived in.

K-Rock hopped up and sat on top of the park bench, beside me. And given the way his eyes drank me in, I wondered what he was thinking, so I just asked him. "Wassup? You okay? Why are you looking at me like that?"

"No reason. You just look real pretty today." He stroked my hair and tucked it behind both ears. "You not the same Icy I used to call my lil sis."

"Well, thank you." I laughed and then said in a playful exhaustion. "I've finally made it outta the lil sis zone."

"Yeah, you grown up now." He flicked my chin.

"I am," I said, waiting for him to follow up with something, anything that would let me know he's wanted to be my knight in the ghetto all along. But he didn't say a word. He just sat there quietly, looking as if he was fumbling through his thoughts.

After a moment of silence that lasted way too long, he said, "I went to see Face the other day."

My chest tensed up, but I played it off by giving K-Rock a careless shrug. "So. And?"

K-Rock looked taken aback. "So? And? Wassup with that? You mad at him or something?"

"Pissed off."

"Why?"

"'Cause I am."

"What he do?" he asked, completely confused.

"He knows what he did."

"Well, fill me in, 'cause when I saw him, he asked me to check on you—"

"So that's why you here? To babysit me for Face?"

"Whoa, I'm not a babysitter and I'm here because I wanted to see you myself."

"Oh, really?"

"Yeah, really. Now finish telling me what your problem is with your brother."

"'Cause it's like Schooly died and they forgot that I existed. Face went to prison. Daddy ran off with a new family to Baltimore. Queenie went to the store and never came back, and I'm stuck here wit' Evilene, queen of the flying monkeys." I paused. Hesitated. Then decided to take a chance and reveal this thought: "And you left me too."

He arched a brow.

I continued, "Yeah, you."

"Icy, I was young and headed for either prison or the grave. Settin' up drug dealers, hustlin' here and there. These streets is grimy. Trust me. And when Face got locked up, I knew I had to bounce and get myself together. And that's what I did." He lifted my chin and locked into my gaze. "But I always thought about you. Always."

He leaned into me just when everything in me told me to daringly give him a kiss, I heard, "Isis!" ring in from the street.

I knew it was Fresh without even having to look. I dropped my head, pulled myself together, and then looked toward the street.

"That's your man?" K-Rock asked.

"Yeah." I hopped off the bench. "I gotta go."

"Be easy."

"I will," I said, as I walked nervously over to Fresh's car. I could only imagine what he probably thought he saw... but oh well...maybe this'll help him get his mind right, make me his girl, and stop playing.

I leaned in through the passenger window. "Hey, baby, wassup? What you doing here?"

He frowned. "Oh, I'm your baby, huh? Wassup? What I'm doing here? What you tryna play me? Who is dude over there? That's your man?"

He pointed over to K-Rock, who was still sitting there watching us.

"That's my homeboy. Psst. Please. He's like a brother to me. I don't have a man."

"Oh, you don't have a man? Oh. A'ight?" Fresh drew in a breath and then hit me with a smirk. "I tell you what, I need you to get in the car now."

I wanted so badly to break into a smile. Fresh's face was filled with jealousy. And green was such a cute color on him. "Now? I wanted to kick it with my friends for a minute."

His jaw clenched. "I said get in. Now."

I held back my smile, as I opened the door and slid in. Fresh immediately raced up the street, made a sharp left, jumped the curb, and pulled into a vacant lot. He shoved his face into mine and gripped my chin. "You tryna play me?"

I snatched my face away. "I understand you mad, but don't grip my face like that unless you tryna get cut."

"Yo." He mushed the tip of his index finger into my forehead, causing my neck to jerk back. "I don't believe you! Here we been cold rockin' it, all month. I put all other chicks to the side and devoted mostly all of my time to you and this is what you do? I don't know who you think you playin' wit'."

"And I don't know who you think you talking to, but it ain't me. So you need to chill and stop trippin'." I swatted his finger away.

"Stop trippin'? I wake up, go to reach for you, and the only thing next to me is a blunt? Word. You don't wake me up? Nothing? You just jet. And then I come over here to see wassup wit' you and you sittin' in the courtyard wit' a dude. That you telling me is just a friend."

"He is. And anyway, look, I'm not about to sweat you. I been layin' up in your crib all month, doing everything for you, and you ain't asked me yet to be your girl. How long did you think I was gon' go for that? I need a commitment or we need to relax."

"Oh, you wanna relax? Is that what you want?"

"No. But I'm not stupid and I'm not getting ready to assume that we a couple and you haven't asked me to be."

"I need to ask you? You already know you my girl."

"I don't know that." I folded my arms across my chest. "Ask me. Write me a note or do something. Otherwise I'm straight single."

Fresh gave me a crooked grin. "A note?" He chuckled a bit. "Saying what?"

"A note asking me if I wanna be your girl and then you put a yes box, a no box, and a maybe box."

"First of all, I'm not about to write you some lame note and if I did, I damn sure wouldn't put a no box or a maybe box."

"And why not?"

"'Cause your only option is to say yes."

"Oh, really?"

"What? You wanna say something else?"

I thought about continuing my stubborn routine, but by the smile that was on my face, there was no need to. So, I slid my arms around his neck and pressed my lips against his. "No, baby. We would only need a yes box."

"I thought so," he said as we started to kiss. "All you better ever tell me is yes…"

26

Walking with a panther

Fresh was everything black love was made of.
Kind.

Gentle.

Caring.

Had his own money.

And from what I could see his feelings for me ran deep. He loved spending time with me and I loved being with him too, but I was starting to miss my crew.

Plus, I was growing tired of Fresh's pager always going off, his house phone constantly ringing, all night long, and the midnight knocks on his apartment door, with random girls kicking, pounding, and begging to get inside.

Although he swore that it was all about me, I wasn't no fool. And one thing I knew for sure, real hustlers didn't have no customers calling their house phones or banging their doors down. Why? 'Cause there was a difference between your crib and your corner. And since I knew my man wasn't sloppy in the streets, it was crystal clear that he had a few other chicks besides me.

And yeah, I knew other chicks was part of the game but still...I didn't like it smeared in my face. So I knew I needed a break. Today.

Fresh and I were in a custom leather boutique called La-Shae's in New York City. He stepped out of the dressing room and the tailor turned him toward a trifold mirror before taking his measurements.

Fresh had donned a black leather kufi, tilted to the left. Dark black and square-shaped shades shielded his eyes. He wore a double-breasted black suit, with the matching vest, and on his feet was black and red British Knights.

"Word to the mother, that whole ensemble is what's up," I said. "You look soooo dope, baby."

Fresh nodded in agreement.

I carried on, "You make the Treacherous Three look like they need to add one more. You even flyer than Colonel Abrams and Kool Moe Dee put together!"

Fresh slid his shades down the bridge of his nose. "What you want?"

"I'm just giving you your props, baby."

"You been kind of quiet since we got here and I think I know what it is."

"What?"

"You want one of these, don't you?"

Umm, no, but I wasn't about to turn down no custom leather suit. "Of course I want one. My baby look fly so I gotta look fly too."

"You ain't said nothin' but a word." Fresh smiled and looked down at the tailor. "I want you to make my girl one of these, but trim her collar in mink."

"Are you serious?" I squealed.

"You know it."

The tailor's assistant took my measurements and I was

grinning from ear to ear. Afterwards, I ran over to Fresh
and hugged him extra tight. "Thank you."

"Anything for my girl."

Fresh paid the tailor and for the next few hours we
strolled through Midtown, where the city streets was filled
with loads of traffic. Yellow taxis honked. Drivers cussed.
Bicycles danced figure eights around the cars. Crowds of
people bustled up and down the sidewalk; and here I was
in the center of it all, carrying more bags than I'd ever carried before. Fresh even let me get some gear for Kamari.

I held Fresh's hand and squeezed it. "You're the best," I
said. "And I'm soooo grateful to have you as my man."

"Thank you, baby," he said.

I continued, "But I wanna tell you something and I
don't want you to get mad. I want you to understand."

"Depends on what it is."

"Promise me you won't get mad."

"You know I'm not gon' promise that."

I sucked in and pushed out a deep breath. "I wanna go
home tonight."

Fresh came to a sudden halt, stopping midway to the
sidewalk. "Go home? For what? Why? I know you not tryna
kick it with that same, punk ass motherfu—"

I placed a finger up to his lips, stopping him mid-
sentence. "I told you K-Rock was a family friend. My
homie. That's it."

He roughly brushed my finger from his lips. "Why you
defending him?"

"'Cause he's like a brother to me."

"Like a brother, and being a brother, are two different
things. And don't ever put your finger up to my mouth
and try and shut me up again." He mushed me on the side
of my forehead.

I took a deep breath. "Look, I been staying with you for a month. But you not my daddy! And I ain't had no curfew and nobody sweatin' me in forever. I'm grown. And it's not that I necessarily wanna go home, but I do wanna hang out on my side of town with my girls. Maybe stop by and see my cousin so I can see wassup with her and give her what I have for Kamari."

"Your cousin? Didn't you just tell me the other day when I picked you up that your cousin was doggin' you? Tellin' your homegirls that you was actin' funny?"

I sucked my teeth. "Why you gotta throw that in my face? She was upset, that's all. But that's my cousin and I miss her and the baby. Plus, I have all this stuff that I really want to give her for Kamari. And I wanna drop it off to her tonight."

"I'll take you to drop it off."

"I don't need you to take me. 'Cause after I see Yvette, I wanna go and chill with my homegirls for a while. And I might come back to your place tonight and I might not."

Fresh's eyes was bloodshot and the veins in his neck bulged, but, surprisingly, he was calm as he said, "If you wanna go, go. You're right, you been staying with me for over a month, and maybe that was too long. So, if you wanna bounce, then step 'cause my hustle damn sure ain't kidnapping. I'm up here taking you out, taking you shopping, showing you a nice time, but you wanna disrespect me and chase some broke hos and they kids around."

"You're going too far and I don't appreciate that!"

"And I don't appreciate you tryna play me for stupid."

"Play you? Ain't nobody tryna play you. If anything I been played by all the chicks who keep calling you and showing up at your door. But did I sweat you about that? What, you think I didn't notice or I didn't know? What, you think I'm some young and stupid broad? You got me messed up."

"You better calm down and lower your voice!"

"And if I don't? Yo, for real, dig, I appreciate everything you've done for me, but you not about to run me. Nah, that's not how I get down and I ain't having that. So, if you got a problem wit' me going to see my crew and my family, then I suggest you deal with that. 'Cause I'm out!" I flipped him the middle finger and, without thinking twice or looking back, I stormed into the subway and quickly hopped on the PATH train.

27

Rebel without a pause

Eight p.m.

At first when I got here, I didn't think that much had changed. I mean, maybe the month on the wall calendar had flipped. The plastic on the sofa was a little more ripped than I remembered. Maybe there was more grease spots and stains on the banana-colored kitchen walls. Maybe even more floor tile was missin' than before.

But so what? There was a lot that was still the same.

Like the aged Crisco can, with the lumpy chicken grease, that sat in the middle of the stove.

The potato plants on the rusty fire escape.

Nana and Mr. Bill's Saturday night groove.

And my crackhead auntie, drunk uncle, and they friends piled up in here.

So never did I expect to walk into my bedroom and find something outright different: Kamari playing with my little cousins and Yvette nowhere to be seen.

Ten p.m.

Almost all the kids who lived here was asleep. Except Kamari, who walked around with a pissy Pamper and screamed about how she was hungry. I gave her a pack of crackers, but I couldn't change her Pamper, because she didn't have any.

Eleven p.m.

I couldn't take Kamari screaming and crying anymore, so I put clothes on her and we walked across the street to the Chinese store for fried chicken wings and a quart of fried rice. Then we headed to the bodega for a pack of Pampers.

Midnight.

I hadn't watched the clock like this since the night Schooly was killed.

Kamari was dry, fed, and asleep in my arms.

Still no Yvette.

Two a.m.

I was on edge with worry but fightin' to keep my eyes open.

Four a.m.

My neck kept jerking from me dozing in and out of sleep, but I was too scared to give up waiting.

Eight a.m.

"And what is you doing here?" Scared me out of my sleep.

My eyes popped open and immediately my gaze sank into Yvette's face. Her mouth dry, creased, and holding a fish frown. Her lips cracked. Ashy. Her head suddenly seem-in' too big for her frail frame. She looked to be at least twenty pounds thinner since my birthday. Her clothes, which she prided on being fitted, were too big.

"I know you heard me," Yvette carried on. "What you doin' here?"

I curled the left corner of my upper lip. "Whatchu mean, what I'm doin' here? I live here. The question is where you been and why you ain't come home last night?"

"For the same reasons you don't come home."

"Listen, I came here to give you some clothes for Kamari and then I wanted to hang out wit' Munch and Cali. But since you ain't come home I ended up having to stay inside all night and watch Kamari."

"What?" She sucked her teeth and flicked a wrist dismissively. "Don't be acting like I needed you to watch my baby. Mph, Nana was here. And another thing, I don't need you to get my baby no clothes and I most def don't need you checkin' up on me."

"Excuse you?"

"You heard me. I don't know why you all in B.I. anyway. Am I sweatin' you about what you out there doin' with Fresh? No. I'm. Not. I mind my business, which is what you need to do."

"Fresh? Fresh don't have nothin' to do with this. This is about my family. Yes, he's my boyfriend and I spend time with him because I'm gettin' to know him, but you're my cousin—"

"Not really. Actually, I'm just a family friend."

I hesitated. For a moment I felt like I'd been sideswiped. "What?" I said, only because, momentarily, I had no other follow-up. I paused again and then continued with, "You straight buggin'. Now I asked you a question: where you been?"

"I don't have to answer to you!" Yvette turned around and stormed out and into the living room. I hopped off the bed and flew behind her, practically stepping on the heels of her sneakers. That's when I spotted Flip standing in the middle of the floor, wearing the same get-up he had on the other day: dirty and too-big jeans and an oversized orange and faded Sunkist tee with the neck stretched from round to oval. And some busted white Chucks.

A million things raced through my mind, including picking up the glass lamp off the end table and pealing Flip's scalp back with it. "Now I know why you ain't come home!" I said to Yvette. "'Cause you was out wit' this nothin'! I can't believe this! Yo' baby here pissy and hungry, but you out chasin' this crackhead—"

"Correct yourself. My man is not a crackhead, first of all—"

"First of all, you don't have a man, you got a junkie!"

"You don't disrespect Flip like that! Ain't nobody talkin' about Fresh!"

"Like I said before, this don't have nothin' to do with Fresh. Right now I'm worried about Kamari—"

"Since when? And why? I pushed her out, not you! So you go back to runnin' the streets wit' yo' notorious drug dealer!"

"What the—wait, you the one told me to go out with him!"

"And when you start listening to everything I tell you to do? You don't have your own mind?"

"You sounding real stupid right now. And I think I know why, 'cause you must be high and you ain't high off weed!"

"Trick, beat it! You don't come at me like that! Ain't nobody high up in here."

"Then why are you lookin' like that? Eyes all bugged out. Lips all ashy."

"Not that I need to explain anything to you, but for your information, I haven't had any sleep since yesterday afternoon!"

"Yeah, I bet. 'Cause you been hittin' that pipe all night!"

"Yo, I ain't gotta keep listening to you. Come on, Flip!"

"Come on, Flip?! Where you runnin' back to? The crack house? You got a daughter in the other room!"

"You need to mind your business. I'm talkin' to my man—"

"Yeah, he's your man now, but in a minute he gon' be your pimp!"

Whap!

Yvette's hand burned across my face so fast that I didn't have a chance to catch my balance, and I hit the floor. Her fist felt like iron as it landed full speed ahead dead in my mouth, and before I could even process what was happening, I'd already jumped up, yanked Yvette into a tussle, and now had her on the floor, doing my best to stomp through her rib cage.

"Get offa her!" Flip snatched me by my hair, placed an arm around my neck, and started choking me.

Wham! Crack! Crack! Crack! Wham! "Let her go!" Nana screamed, beating Flip in the head with a metal broom handle. Once Nana forced Flip to let me go, she stood in between us. "What in the devil is going on here?! I swear for God, y'all not about to tear up my apartment!" She looked over at me. "Yo' sleazy behind been gone for over a month, and this is the hell you come back in here with?!"

"I didn't do anything! Your granddaughter, Yvette, is runnin' around here smokin' crack, don't you see that?!"

"You lyin' on me!" Yvette screamed.

"SHUT UP!" Nana yelled. "She ain't smokin' no crack! If anybody out in the street doing God knows what, it's you! Runnin' in and outta here like you grown, like I ain't responsible for you!"

"Responsible for me? Really? Since when you start caring about me or anything that got to do with me?"

"I took you in when your mama and your daddy didn't want you!"

"And I probably would've been better off had you just sent me to a foster home! 'Cause living here ain't nothin' but hell. You ain't never did nothin' for me but cuss me out. All my clothes I had to beg, borrow, and wait for Yvette to steal 'em! All you ever done for me was give me a bunch of grief! So you can save all that, 'cause the last thing you did for me was a favor."

"You better shut yo' mouth!"

"No, I won't. *You* need to stop talkin' to me. And you need to focus on the newest crackhead livin' up in your house, 'cause soon as he finish turnin' her out, she'll be walkin' out and leavin' the baby behind for good."

"The devil is a liar and your wicked behind just came here to steal, kill, and destroy! You just an ingrate. A nothin'! A unruly spirit up! And I ain't gon' have you in my house, talking trash to me! Now get out! Go back to whatever gutter you crawled out from 'cause you are no longer welcomed in this here!"

"I don't care! What you think I need you or I need to stay here? Screw you! I'm good and, Yvette, when he turn you out and have you beatin' that concrete don't even look for me! 'Cause I'm through witchu!"

28

Black steel in a moment of chaos

"*Isis,*" *Queenie called my name, as she leaned against my door frame.*

"*Yeah.*" *I sat in my wicker throne chair and stared at my Whodini poster. "What?"*

"*Don't what me. I gotta run out. And I want you to go downstairs to your nana's for a while.*"

"*Why I gotta go down there? I don't like it down there.*"

"*Don't question me! You do what I tell ya to do!*"

"*I'll wait for you in my room. They didn't even come to Schooly's funeral and you want me to chill wit' 'em? I'll pass.*"

"*What did I just say?!*"

"*No, I'm not goin'!*"

Whap! "*Who are you talkin' to like that? Huh? I'm tired of telling you to do something and you telling me what you is and ain't gon' do! Now I said get your behind downstairs!*" *She snatched me out of the chair. "And before you even ask, no you can't come with me! I need a minute to think, so I'm goin' to get me a Pepsi and hang out for a little while...."*

"When you comin' back?"

"Icy? Wassup? You a'ight?"

I sat in the courtyard, on the park bench, my knees pulled into my chest, with my eyes closed, lost in a memory.

"Wassup? What's wrong?"

I opened my eyes and tears slid out from the corners and rolled down my cheeks. K-Rock, who stood in front of me, wiped my tears away and said, "Wassup? What happened to you?"

Despite the left side of my face aching, somehow I managed to smile. "I'm a'ight. I'm good." I sniffed. "Wassup with you?"

He sat down beside me, dropping his gym bag on the ground. "You lyin' to me now? I thought we were better than that? And evidently, if you out here crying with your lip swollen and busted, then the last thing you are, is a'ight."

I swallowed, did my best to shake my thoughts and let 'em go. I could feel tears knocking at the backs of my eyes again. "I'm straight. I promise you."

"You makin' false promises now?" K-Rock looked around the half-empty courtyard, filled only with old junkies, new dealers, and a few dudes sprinkled on the basketball court. "Did somebody out here say somethin' or do somethin' to you?"

I shook my head. The tears were now making their way back to the corners of my eyes and then without warning they fell along the sides of my nose and over my lips.

"Ya man?" K-Rock said, extra hyped. "Yo, what he do?

He put his hands on you? Where he at? And you better tell me, 'cause I promise you, he won't touch you again."

"No. He didn't do nothin' to me."

"Then tell me! 'Cause I swear to God, seeing you like this is making me mad as hell!"

"It's a lot." I shrugged. "That's it."

"What you mean, it's a lot?"

"It just seems like the more time goes on, the worse things get for me."

"Like what?"

"Like my grandmother threw me out! Told me I had to go and don't ever come back."

"She threw you out? What? Are you serious?"

"What you think I'ma joke about something like that? Yeah, I'm serious."

"Why would she do that? You're only sixteen, where does she think you s'pose to go? She didn't mean that. She couldn't've."

"You think she cares?" I wrinkled my brow. "All that old, fat, and nasty broad cares about is Mr. Bill and Jesus."

"So this is about Mr. Bill?" He looked taken aback. "Or Jesus?"

"No. This is about Nana never giving a damn. Never talkin' to us. Always talkin' at us. Cussin' us out. Never buyin' us nothin'. Me and Yvette looked like straight dirty girls until Yvette figured out how to boost and not get caught." I flung the tears that continued to flow down my face.

"Listen." He draped his arm over my shoulders, pulling me along the side of his chest. "Maybe you should chill with me for a minute and perhaps by the end of the day, your grandmother will have cooled off and you two can talk about it. 'Cause real rap, ain't nothin' out here in these streets and you know that. So you need to make amends and go home."

"So what you sayin' is that I should beg? I'll sleep outside on this bench first." I took his arm from around me and sat up straight. "Never. I ain't never speakin' to her again. And she better not ever need nothin' from me! I wouldn't care if she was on fire 'cause I wouldn't even spit on her. And Yvette, I promise you, I'ma kill her. And I put that on everything."

"Yo, what? Yvette? Wassup with that? That's your girl. Your cousin. Why you trippin' like that? Cousins fight all the time. Y'all need to squash that beef."

"Psst. Please. She did this to my face and I tried to stomp her until her crackhead lungs collapsed."

"Crackhead? Yvette?"

"Yeah, Yvette. Dirty-ass Flip been messin' wit' her since we was little. Kamari is his baby and everything."

"I can't believe that."

"Believe it. And in a minute she gon' be a straight alleyway broad, turning tricks for a hit. I already see it. And Nana wanna play dumb, 'cause Flip probably stealing and paying her so he and Yvette can get high there and Kamari—" I stopped mid-sentence, my words suddenly caught up in the grip of the iron fist wedged into my throat.

I looked around and the courtyard was filled with more people. Some folks headed to work and a few more dealers taking their place on the concrete.

K-Rock kissed me on my forehead and said, "Look, you can't sit here like this and plus you need some ice on your face. So why don't you come over to my crib?"

I squinted, surprised at his suggestion.

"Don't be looking at me like that. What, you can't hang

out with me on my side of town for a while? What else you got to do? Or you tryna stay here and make yourself comfortable on this park bench?"

I chuckled. "You already know the answer to that."

"Then let's go. And no dissin' the Batmobile, either," he said, as we walked up on a dark brown Rabbit hatchback, with a black passenger door, and purple tinted windows. If my mouth wasn't so sore I would've fallen out in laughter. Instead my eyes danced in delight.

K-Rock placed the key in the ignition and then looked at me like he could read my thoughts. "Knock it off." He laughed, as he took off up the street. "I don't have that hustle dough anymore. I'ma college boy and right about now that means I'm—"

"Broke."

"Saving my money." He gave me a playful frown. "You tryna play me?"

"Never."

"I'm just checkin', 'cause see the difference in the money I had then and the money I have now isn't really the amount—it's the risk associated with it. I don't have to wake up in prison, somebody tryna put a gun to my head, or worse, dead."

"Boy, that's life."

"It don't have to be. It's a whole world out here and er'body ain't tryna get drug money or be a stick-up artist."

"Everybody got a hustle. It's just a matter of the one you choose. You trying to go to school, for what? To hustle for somebody else? To take the dough they think you should have? I mean, I'm not exactly knocking this college thing. I'm just saying that if you make more money on the block, then I don't see the need to leave."

"Icy, you gotta stop thinking like that. It's a lot out here and just because you go to a nine to five everyday doesn't mean you can't get what you want." K-Rock pulled into a small driveway that sat alongside a red brick house with black shutters and a screened-in porch.

"You live here?" I looked around at the tree-lined street, the flowers in the front yards, and the freshly manicured lawns.

"Yeah." He got out the car and opened my door. "Now come in, let me introduce you to my father and step-mother."

My eyes grew wide. "This is where you're from or did you just move here? And father and stepmother? Where's your real mother? And I can't meet them, looking like this. You can't be serious!"

"Would you relax? Chill. One thing at a time. My father and stepmother raised me."

"Really?"

"Yeah, when I was two, I got shot by a stray bullet."

I gasped.

"Yeah." He nodded. "Popped in the chest, a few inches from my heart. I could've died. It scared my dad, and since my mother couldn't afford to move, I went to live with him and I been here ever since."

"So how did you get to Da Bricks?"

"My mother lives around the corner. I used to spend weekends with her and on one of those weekends, I met Face. We became friends and you know the rest. Now are we gon' sit out here in the car while you interview me or are you gon' come in the house?"

"I can't go in your house looking like this. I don't want your parents thinking I'm some sort of ghetto-hood-skeezer or somethin'."

K-Rock pulled in and pushed out a deep breath. "Look, after I introduce you to my parents, when and if they ask you what happened, just tell them you were hanging out at the gym with me, you were playing around with the boxing bag, when it swung back and hit you in the face. They won't ask any more questions after that."

"You sure?"

"Positive."

I followed K-Rock, and the moment we walked into his house, his parents, who were sitting on a black leather couch talking, both stopped and looked over at me. His father cracked a half a smile and his stepmother looked at me with concern. "What happened to you, baby?" she asked before K-Rock could even introduce me.

"Umm." I hesitated.

"She was hanging out with me at the gym and the boxing bag swung back—"

"Say no more," his father said. "That has happened to me one too many times."

"Told you," K-Rock mumbled. "Anyway, Ma, Dad, this is Isis. A friend of mine. These are my parents."

"Nice to meet you, Isis," his stepmother said. "But I think you better let Ke'Ron take you into the kitchen and give you some ice for your face."

"Thank you." I looked over at K-Rock. "Come on, *Ke'Ron*. I need some ice please."

He laughed, as we headed into the kitchen. He dumped a tray of ice cubes into a plastic bag and handed it to me, and then we settled in his room, which was located in the basement. It was cool though. There was a full-size bed, a small green leather couch, and a floor-model TV, and on the walls were wood shelves that held boxing medallions and tons of trophies.

"How long have you been boxing?" I asked, taking a seat on the edge of his bed.

"Since I was nine." He turned the television on and *Sanford and Son* filled the screen.

"That's amazing. So you must love it."

"It's cool."

"You know what I've always wanted to do? And don't laugh." I pointed a finger at him.

"What?"

"Ice-skate." I pinched the ends of my T-shirt and swayed from side to side. "I used to love imagining that I was on the ice, skating, and dancing effortlessly in my tutu."

"Word? Have you ever ice-skated?"

"No. Daddy promised to take me, but it never happened."

"I'll take you."

"For real?" I squealed.

"Yeah. When I come back home for Thanksgiving, I'll come scoop you and we'll go ice-skating."

"That would be so dope."

"Yeah, it would be." He stared at me and I knew a million things were on his mind.

"Whatchu thinking?" I asked him.

"About I wish your life was different."

I shrugged. "These are the breaks."

"It can change though. You gotta believe that life can be different. That it's okay to dream about more than gettin' money in the streets."

"K-Rock—excuse me, Ke'Ron—please. Don't turn into a just-say-no commercial on me. I'm really not in the mood for you to sweat me like that."

"You need to learn to listen sometime."

"And I don't wanna hear that either. It's only ten o'clock in the morning and already I've had a long day. I don't know where I'ma live. I don't have no money. Nothing. Therefore, this whole 'life is what you make it, all you gotta do is believe it' nonsense is that last thing I wanna hear. So, save the lectures please."

"I'm not lecturing you. I'm tryna save you."

"But I don't need you to be Superman, Clark Kent. I already have a man."

"Oh, word." I can tell by how he said that I'd pissed him off. "Where your man at now? 'Cause I don't see him. And you worried about Yvette getting turned out—from where I'm sitting you better make sure your man don't end up trying to be your pimp."

I felt like he'd just drop-kicked me. "What? I can't believe you just said that to me! What, you think you better than me, 'cause you living out here in the suburbs and all you cut out to do is play hood? Here I thought you was a real dude and all this time you looking down on me!"

"Don't come at me like that. Hood is the last thing I play. You already seen me in the street so don't test me. And look down on you? You my people. My little sister—"

"If I hear that again I'ma scream!"

He continued, as if he hadn't heard a word that I said. "And you know I wouldn't never look down on you!"

"All I know is what I see."

"So you don't trust me?"

"I don't trust nobody." Ugg! I hated that tears were sneaking back into my eyes. "You know what, I need to get outta here." I stood up. "Take me back to Da Bricks. I need to go."

"Listen." K-Rock looked up at me. "Sit down. You ain't

goin' nowhere right now. You know I wasn't trying to start no argument witchu, I was just trying to tell you something you needed to hear."

"Well, I don't wanna hear it right now."

"Cool. I'll be quiet." He tossed me the remote. "Find us a movie. I'ma go upstairs and pop us some popcorn." He leaned toward me and kissed me on the forehead, and as he attempted to follow up with a kiss on the cheek, I turned my face and his lips landed on mine. He didn't flinch or move his lips. He soaked the moment in and then whispered, "We can't do that."

I swear I wanted to slap him. I was soooooo sick of this lil sis, protector routine. "A'ight," I said, leaning back on his bed, and pressing the remote. "It's not that we can't. It's that you won't."

"Exactly," he said as he left the room.

29

She caught

"I know I was buggin'," I said to Yvette, walking into our bedroom and sitting Indian style on my bed. I knew I was takin' a chance being here so soon. But Nana was locked up in her room with Mr. Bill, so I was safe—well, as safe as I could be around here.

Besides, I ain't have no place else to go, so there was no choice but to call a truce.

"Yeah." Yvette twisted her lips and rolled her eyes. "You was outta control."

"And what about you? Don't even try it. It was not all me."

"Most of it was." She hesitated. "I guess I played my part. But still, you came at me first and I had to defend myself. Calling me a crackhead and saying that I just jetted and didn't come back for my baby."

I looked Yvette over. Her eyes were clear and her lips no longer looked cracked and ashy. One side of her mouth was swollen, but that came from me socking her in it. "So, maybe I was wrong for calling you a crackhead. But I thought you looked high. You gotta admit you lost some weight."

"Yes. I did. Thank you. I did have a baby."

"Three years ago, though."

"Yeah, and my stomach was still fat. So I went on a diet. You been gone for a straight month so of course you gon' notice it right away."

"Maybe. It was just seeing you next to Flip, knowing he a crackhead, and knowing that he too freakin' old and dirty to even be around you."

"There you go again. Whether you like it or not, he's Kamari's father and I'm not gon' exclude him from her life. I don't have a father, and I'm not gon' let Kamari go through what I went through."

"But he a junkie." I frowned.

"You don't know that!"

"I saw him coppin' the other day when I was out there with Cali. Who, by the way, said you be doggin' me left and right."

Yvette smirked. "Number one, I don't even get down wit' Cali like I used to because she runs her freakin' mouth tooooo much. Even Munch said she don't never shut up. So unless you hear it directly from me, don't listen to nothin' Cali gotta say. And number two, yes, Flip copped earlier today, because in order to get into a detox program you gotta have drugs in your system. But he didn't get high to get high. And for your information, that's why he was here today. Because he leaving for the program and wanted to see Kamari before he left."

"So why was you out all night with him?"

"Same reason you spend the night with yo' man. Like I said earlier today, do I question you about Fresh?"

I paused. "Yo, what is it with you and Fresh? You the one who told me to go out with him. You told me specifically that you was cool with me being with him. And now that I'm with him, and I like him, spending time with him, you tryna play me out. You act like you jealous."

"Jealous? Of what? You and Fresh? Never that."

"Then why you trippin'?"

"You trippin'. For the last month, you been riding his jock. Like seriously, for real, can I get my cousin back?"

"I'm here. I never went anywhere. Fresh didn't take me away from you."

"I can't tell."

"Yvette. We family. And blood or no blood, you like a sister to me. and I wouldn't never play you, and especially not for no dude."

"It didn't look that way to me."

"Well, that's how it is. And truthfully, sometimes you just gotta get outta this hell hole. And it's like ever since I been with Fresh I feel like I can breathe better. I can't stand being closed up in here."

"Me either, but right now, this is all I got. Maybe when I get eighteen I can get my own spot, but until then, this is where I'm at."

"I can't do it. Always gotta watch yo' back. Always on guard. Can't ever really get no sleep. Nana always cussin' you out when she feels like it."

"Nana is crazy. Like looney. Don't you know after you left—"

"You mean, after she threw me out."

"Yeah. After that, she cussed Flip all the way out and told him had she known for sure he was Kamari's father when she was first born that she would've had his black behind locked up."

"She said that?"

"Yes. And she told him if he ever put his hands on any of her granddaughters again that she was gon' slice his throat."

I smiled. "Nana took up for me?"

"Word is bond. And that's when I looked at Flip and told him that if me and my cousin is fightin' that he needs to mind his business, 'cause he had no right gettin' in it."

I stretched across my bed and fell out laughing. I laughed so hard my stomach started to hurt. "Yoooo, Yvette, remember when we were little and Queenie sent us outside with that blade and a lock and sock?"

Yvette walked over to my bed and sat Indian style next to me. "Heck yeah, I remember. We was 'bout to piss in our panties."

"Not me. Maybe you was. I was thorough."

"You ain't become thorough until you left her face open."

I snickered. "True."

"Isis." Yvette leaned against me and placed her head on my shoulder. "I'm sorry I got mad at you and, instead of telling you that I missed you, I went off. I shouldn't have ever put my hands on you."

"I'm sorry too, Yvette, and all we got, for real, is each other. You my homegirl, my sister, and Kamari is my niece. I love you two. And nothin' and nobody gon' ever come between us."

"I feel the same way," she said.

"So we straight. We good?" I asked.

"We gon' always be good."

"Cool." I pulled one of Fresh's blunts from my pocket and handed it to her. "Now let's go out on the roof, so we can spark that up."

30

I used to let the mic smoke

Thoughts of Fresh haunted my sleep. I missed my baby, terribly. And I couldn't go another day without seeing him. We had to make up. I straight needed us back together. And hopefully he felt the same way—like he was still diggin' me and didn't wanna dismiss me.

I eased outta bed. "Yvette," I whispered.

No answer.

I called her name again, "Yvette."

Nothing.

I walked over to her bed and she wasn't there, only Kamari, who was sucking her thumb and sleeping.

My heart dropped to the pit of my stomach.

Breathe.

Breathe.

Maybe it ain't what it seems.

Chill.

Chill.

Relax.

Don't jump to no conclusions.

I sat back down on the edge of my bed, holding my face in my hands. "Oh my God," I mumbled, as visions of Yvette being with Flip filled my mind.

"Isis, you a'ight?" I whipped around and faced the door. Yvette was standing there with a white plastic bag in her hand. "What's wrong with you?" she asked. "Why you looking like that?"

"Where you comin' from?"

"The bodega across the street." She swung the bag, making the plastic rustle. "Kamari needed some Pampers." She paused. "Oh, what, you thought I was out coppin'?" She laughed.

"Oh, you think that's funny?" I sucked my teeth.

"No, actually I think it's stupid."

I snickered. "Whatever."

Yvette plopped down on her bed. "Guess who I just saw?" She took the pack of Pampers from the bag and shoved it under her bed.

"Who?"

"Your original crush groove, K-Rock."

Given, yesterday, when he wouldn't even kiss me back, and last night, when he dropped me off and barely said two words to me, I was doing everything in my power not to smile. "Psst, please. Ain't nobody thinking about him."

"Umm hmm." Yvette twisted her lips.

"Well, maybe you are, but I'm not."

"I bet."

"I'm not. I mean, he's okay. Cute. Sexy. But he's no longer my type and he only sees me as a little sister. That's it."

"Yeah, that's what his mouth says, but when you wasn't

around, he would ask about you. He was lookin' real disappointed. I know too many"—she made invisible quotes—"brothers that interested in what their sisters are doing."

"I hear you, but trust me. It's nothin'."

"A'ight, well, he asked me about you this morning and I told him you was up here asleep. 'Cause that's what I thought."

"And what he say?"

"He smiled and just said to tell you he was at the gym and hopefully, he would catch you later."

"I don't know what he telling you to tell me that for."

"'Cause he wanna see you and you wanna see him too."

"No, I don't." I hopped off the bed.

"Then where you goin'?"

"I need to shower and get dressed. I got something I need to do."

"Umm hmm." She twisted her lips. "I betchu do."

I knew I should've ran back out the door, instead of listening to the stupid voice in my head—or maybe it was my heart—telling me to show up here. When I saw K-Rock shadowboxing in the ring, it completely turned me on.

I had a man and I needed to stop sweatin' this one.

K-Rock was dressed in silky black boxing shorts with red stitches on the waistband and a black tank that dripped over his eight-pack like ebony paint. Some man, who I guess was his coach, stood ringside and quietly watched K-Rock's technique.

I took a seat and faced the ring.

K-Rock tossed a punch left. A left hook, an uppercut right. Then he followed up with a jab. His face was super serious. He was definitely in his zone.

I watched him for at least five minutes, and my heart thundered with each air punch he threw.

Ugg! This is sooooooo stupid. I need to get outta here.

I quickly hopped out of my seat and rushed to the door.

"Yo!" came from behind me. "You give up that easy?"

I stopped in my tracks. Turned around. "I didn't know I had anything to give up. I just came to check you out for a minute. I saw you. And now I'm leaving."

"But I don't want you to leave."

Am I blushing?

I think I'm blushing.

Oh my God, I'm blushing!

Ugg. I felt sooooooo stupid.

K-Rock stepped out of the ring and walked over to me. He kissed me on my forehead and said, "I'm happy to see you."

"Really?"

We took a seat in the back of the gym. "Whatchu mean, really? I'm always happy to see you." He paused. "Oh, wait, you still mad about yesterday? Yo, listen to me, I know we got a connection. I feel it too, but you too young for me right now."

I couldn't believe he said that. My heart was thundering. "What, you think I'm trying to get with you? Psst, please you really are like a brother to me."

"But you kissed me."

"That was a mistake."

"Why you lyin'? Now I'ma ask you this straight out: do you like me?"

Lie. Lie. Don't tell him. Just lie.

I looked into his eyes and said, "Yeah. I do."

"And I'm checkin' for you too."

I blinked. Three times. "What did you just say?"

"I said, I'm checkin' for you too. I always have been, but you were always too young and you're still too young."

"I'm not a kid. I'm grown."

"You're only sixteen. I'm twenty. In college and I can't chill with you like I really want to. Not yet. I just can't."

I felt like such a fool. "Look, I gotta go."

"Why? You don't wanna hang out a little bit? I'm getting ready to get outta here."

Now I was pissed. "Hang out? You trippin'. Now you think I should chill with you? Didn't you just have me admit my feelings, but instead of making future plans, you turned around and walked me back to the little-sister zone. What, you a comedian now? You tryna be funny? I don't have time to play with you."

"Isis."

"I gotta go." He grabbed me by the hand and twirled me into his chest.

"I'm goin' back to school tomorrow." He placed a kiss on the side of my neck.

"I need you to stop."

"I know. I need to. I do." He kissed me again. "But I just want you to know that I'm never too far away if you need me."

"I gotta go."

"I know." He kissed me on my forehead.

I took a step back, turned, and walked away.

31

Bootleg

"**G**et in." Stopped me dead in my tracks, as I walked out of the community center and headed up the block. "Now." It was Fresh, peering at me through the passenger-side window. "Don't make me say it again."

My heart dropped and I looked up and down the street. Nobody was really out here other than a few winos and fiends. Even the bus stops was empty.

"Oh, I see." He nodded. "You tryna test me."

"I didn't say that." I rolled my eyes and tried to ignore my heart thundering in my chest. "What?" I sighed as I slid into his car and slammed the door.

"I got your damn what." Fresh pressed the tips of his fingers into my temple, pinning the side of my face against the tinted window.

"What the hell is wrong with you?!" I grabbed his wrist and tried to snatch his hand off of me, but I couldn't. Instead, it felt like I was trying to move a thousand-pound piece of steel. He pressed his fingers deeper into my skin.

"Get offa me!" I screamed, flailing my arms, then taking my hands and slapping him across his face.

"Stop," he said sternly.

"Get offa me! What is your problem?!" I screamed, still unable to break free. "Move!" I swung with all my might, raking my fingers down the side of his face.

"Didn't I tell you to stop!" Fresh took his free hand, grabbed both of mine and now I was frozen. He peeked into the rearview mirror at his face and spat, "You lucky you ain't break my skin."

"No," I snapped. "You lucky I ain't break your skin, but let my hands go and see what I'ma do for you!"

"What you better do is stop talking all slick and answer my damn question. Now where you been? 'Cause the last time I seen or heard from you, you left me in the middle of New York City like some sucker you can straight play with. You lucky I don't bust you upside your head. Or make you strip and give me these clothes back. Matter of fact, I should take back everything I bought you, since you think you can just hop up and do what you wanna do."

"You ain't my father! I'm grown. Nobody tells me what the hell to do!"

"Oh, you grown, huh? Keep on tryna front and play with that cocky attitude and I'ma end up hurtin' you."

"What you think you doin' now?" I wiggled, trying to free myself again.

"Stop movin'. I swear to God, Isis. I don't wanna hurt you so you need to stop talkin' like you done lost your mind. I'm not the one. 'Cause I'm crazy and I'll show you crazy."

I wanted to explode. But I knew by the look on Fresh's face that I needed to relax. "Get offa me..." I paused. "Please."

"And why should I do that?"

"So I can have a chance to talk to you."

"I swear to God, when I let you go, if you hit me, jump out the car, or say something slick, I'ma handle you." Fresh lifted his hands and shot me a look that clearly told me not to try him.

I sucked my teeth as I massaged my temples and then my wrists. I flipped down the visor and looked at my face in the mirror. My temples were slightly red. I looked back over to Fresh. "I don't believe we even going through this."

Silence.

"Fresh, baby, look. I was mad and maybe I overreacted, but you was giving me grief about me simply wanting to hang out with my crew and see my cousin. That's all I wanted to do. I was gon' come back to your spot."

"Nah, I felt like you tried to play me like a john. Like a sucker. Leaving me in the middle of the street after I done spent my money on you. And then days go by and you don't even come and see me, I gotta come lookin' for you."

"I was gon' come and see you today. But I need you to understand that my life is complicated right now. My family is a mess."

"I should be considered your family."

What did he just say? I smiled, laughed. "Boy, you so crazy. I like that, but we ain't family yet." I lifted my left hand and wiggled my ring finger. "Soon though."

Fresh shook his head and cracked a crooked grin. "You want a ring? You gon' have to calm that mouth. I ain't gon' have no wife talking crazy to me. And either you gon' learn on your own that you don't have to be so smart and spicy all the time. Or you gon' mess around and make me teach you. Now I'ma ask you this again, and don't lie. Where you been?"

I took a deep breath. *Relax. You got this.* "I been here chillin' with my cousin and my crew. That's it."

"Didn't I just tell you not to lie? What you think I'm stupid? You think I don't know what time it is?"

I huffed. "I just told you what time it is!"

He shot me a look. "You better calm down."

"I'm trying to be calm."

"Check it, was you out with some other dude?"

"You trippin'. Hard. Real hard. I just told you what I was doin'."

"You been chillin' wit' K-Rock?"

My heart dropped to my stomach. "What are you talkin' about?"

"Don't even try and run game. 'Cause if that's where you been and who you been kickin' it to, then you can get him to buy you clothes and take care of you."

"Like I told you before, K-Rock is my brother. That's it, my brother. It ain't nothin' like that. He's a friend of the family and he's been around ever since I was like ten years old."

"That ain't what your cousin said."

"What?" I hesitated. "My cousin? She been runnin' her mouth, again? Word is bond, you already know she likes you, and she's jealous of me. She's the one who wanted to get with you in the beginning. But I'ma tighten her up. You can put money on that." I nodded. Drifted off into thought and then looked back over to Fresh. "I don't wanna talk about Yvette no more. We need to talk about me and you."

"Yeah, let's talk about me and you 'cause I ain't see you in a minute."

"Look, trust me. Believe me on this: I'm not playing you. I care about you. I like being with you and everything, but sometimes I just be needing a minute to think, without you sweatin' me or thinking I'm not coming back. Because I'm here with you. And I really wanna see where this relationship goes."

He looked me over. His eyes taking me in from head to toe. "All I'ma say is if I find out you playin' me, that's it, I'm not dealing with you no more."

"It's not like that. I promise you." I slid my arms around his neck and pressed my lips against his.

"So you coming home with me, right?"

"Of course, papi."

"A'ight, that's all I been wantin' to hear."

32

Top billin'

The last two weeks had been heaven. Me and Fresh had been gettin' along perfectly, without arguing, fighting, or me feeling like I needed to leave. There was something bothering me though. I needed to have my own money. I didn't like depending on him for everything.

I was a hustler and I needed to make my own dough, not have it rationed out to me.

I turned off the burner and slid the cheese omelet I just made for Fresh onto a plate. Then I buttered his toast and sat it on a saucer beside his orange juice.

I usually sat on his lap while he ate, but not today. Today, I sat across the table from him.

Fresh looked at me and his eyes glowed. I knew that he loved me. And I loved him, so I was hoping, praying even, that when I told him what I needed, he would give it to me.

"Fresh."

"Wassup, baby. Why you sittin' over there? Come sit next to me."

"I'll come over there in a minute."

"What's wrong?"

"I need to ask you something."

"Speak."

I hesitated. *Just say it. Breathe in. Breathe out and just say it.* "Do you think you can front me a few ounces of weed, something small, like a QP?"

Fresh blinked and practically dropped the food out of his mouth. "Repeat that?"

"*I said*, 'Do you think you can front me a few ounces of weed, something small like a QP?' "

A smile ran across his face. "Baby, it's a difference in weighing out and baggin' up weed and selling it."

"I know that."

"So then tell me, what you know about selling weed? QP? Four ounces?" he said with a smirky grin. "How you gon' handle that?"

"Boy, please." I waved my hand and beamed with pride. "Shiiiiit, I know about making a dollar. Always have. I been down by law since the day I was born. My mama taught me how to hustle without selling my body."

"Word?"

"Word."

"Okay, well, we gon' see. I'ma front you a QP."

"For real?" I said, excited.

"Yeah. Now, keep in mind that you my girl, but this is business. And you gon' have to bring me back what you gon' owe me."

"Oh, you will get your money."

"I tell you what, bring me back half of what you gon' owe me and keep the rest. Now where you gon' sell this weed at?"

"Well, I know I can get it sold in school."

"School? Do you know what kind of chance you taking slingin' in a school? How you gon' make that work?"

"I'ma run it just like the block. I'ma get me a crew and set up shop."

"But school ain't for another two weeks."

"I know. So for now I can sell some to my homegirls and to a few people I know around the way and in the park. And when school starts, I'ma take another four ounces and knock it off."

"You got big dreams."

I winked. "And that's what you love about me."

"True. But school? You know they do searches at school."

"And? So? I told you I'ma hustler and I can do this."

"A'ight, young girl, show me."

"As you like to say, 'You ain't said nothin' but a word.'"

"Bet. So when you gon' start?"

"Today. I'ma bag it up and I betchu I'll be back with your money in less than five hours."

"I'll spot you six."

33

The vapors

Pink and black Air Jordans. Check.

A small waist pouch to keep my weed in. Check.

Two-tone Levi's jeans with solid black on one side, and black and white stripes on the other. Check.

A white off-the-shoulder, airbrushed T-shirt with *Fly Girl* sprayed across it. Check.

Lookin' ill and feelin' great. Check. Check.

I walked out of the bedroom and into the living room, where Fresh sat looking at his pager. I leaned over him from behind the couch and planted a kiss on his lips.

"Be easy out there, baby. And watch your back. Oh, and take my little hoopty. The Chevette. You can't be gettin' on no bus."

I grinned from ear to ear. "Thank you, baby." I took the keys from his hand.

"A'ight." He held his fist up and I gave him a bump. "The clock is tickin'."

I pulled up to Da Bricks and practically entered Nana's apartment skippin'. She was standing at the stove stirring grits when she looked at me and did a double take. "I don't know what you so goddamn happy about. Maybe you high or you done robbed somebody or somethin', but I'ma tell you right now, leave the devil outside and don't come up in here startin' nothin'."

I didn't respond to that. I just kept on going to the bedroom, where Yvette was. I pushed the door open and Yvette jumped. Her eyes sprung open in surprise as she shoved something under her pillow and hopped up. She frowned. "Oh, I see you decided to show up. What? Fresh let you out?"

"You know what, I told myself on my way over here that I was gon' try and let this jealous mess and your smart comments go. But don't push me. And by the way, don't think Fresh didn't tell me how you told him that I was hanging out with K-Rock. I don't appreciate that, but I'ma let it slide. For now."

She rolled her eyes and huffed. "Whatchu want? I'm busy."

I smiled. "I gotta show you somethin'." I reached in my pouch and pulled out two sandwich baggies full of nickel bags of bud.

"What's that?" Yvette asked, unimpressed.

"What you think it is? This is our way outta here! This is the plan. We gon' sell this at the park, and when school starts up, we gon' open up shop there. Get our crew, Munch and Cali, we gon' each take a floor, whatever floor your homeroom is on, is gon' be where you sling. We gon' run the school like the block."

"And you gon' get it in school, knowing they got security and metal detectors."

I smiled and rubbed my hands together. "Peanut butter and jelly, baby."

"What?"

"I'ma pack half-empty jars of peanut butter with sandwich bags of weed. Security is not about to look all through the jar, digging through peanut butter."

"The smell?"

"Won't be no smell. The peanut butter absorbs it."

Yvette smirked and clapped her hands. "Bra.Vo. Sounds like you and Fresh got this all worked out."

"This don't have nothing to do with Fresh. He just the connect, so to speak. And after a while, and we re-up and sell out a few times, before you know it, you gon' have enough money so that you and Kamari can get your own crib before you turn even eighteen."

"Did I ask you to go apartment huntin' for me? No, I don't think I did."

I rolled my eyes to the ceiling. "Look, I'm trying to help you out, so you can get this money."

"So now I'm s'pose to work for you?"

"This ain't about you working for me. This is about money. And about having a better hustle than stealing clothes out the mall, 'cause judging by your gear lately, that ain't going that great."

"Oh, now you wanna put me down? You ain't say all that when I was boosting for me *and you*, so we could have something fly to wear to school. I ain't hear you runnin' your mouth then, but now you think you better than me!"

"I'm not trying to put you down!" I snapped. "I'm not even trying to argue with you. I'm trying to help you out and maybe you can have a better life to take care of Kamari."

"No thank you. I don't know why you *alllllllll* of a sudden you're so worried about me and Kamari. It ain't like we've seen you in the past two weeks. And now you wanna come up in here tryna sell me some pipe dreams!"

"The word pipe is probably the last word that need to be comin' outta your mouth. But you know what, I'm not gon' beg you. Drugs sell themselves. So either you down or you not."

"I'm down, but it ain't witchu. I got my own hustle and maybe you too good for it now, but it's working for me. So you step off with your so-called dreams and your fake ambition. Runnin' around here like Fresh is the president. But I don't need you, Fresh, or that whack-ass weed."

"Know what? I'm finished with you. You got problems and I can't solve 'em."

"I didn't ask you to. Now, good-bye. Leave. Up in here tryna pimp me."

"Pimp you? Mph, no, I won't be pimpin' you. Flip gon' handle that."

34

Dying to move

Funky fresh, dressed to impress, ready to party... blasted from the deejay's turntable as I glided into the park, nodding my head to the music and refusing to let thoughts of Yvette wreck my flow.

The sun was shining, the park was packed, and as usual this was the place to be. The B-boys were doing their thing on the cardboard, the D-boys were shootin' dice. The basketball court was in the midst of a pick-up game, and everybody else was just chillin' and vibing to the music.

"What's up, sexy?" The deejay smiled and nodded his head at me.

I smiled back, and swayed a little to the tune he'd just dropped. "I'm just chillin', listening to the music, trying to see what you over here doing." I put a little extra boom in my bop, to make it seem like his deejaying was just that crazy. "Do you scratch?"

"Do I?" He showcased his skills.

"Yo, that was stupid fresh. Straight ill. You did that."

He grinned. "So what you got goin' on?"

"Well, right now I'm checking you out, tryna see what you about."

He blushed. "Well, if you hand over them digits, then you can get to know me."

I rocked to the beat for a moment. I knew if I could get the deejay to buy a few bags of bud from me, then the rest would be gravy. Especially since the deejay was the heart of the party, and if he liked me and my weed, then I knew it was only a matter of time before he rounded up some clientele for me.

"I tell you what, cat daddy. I'll drop them digits for you after you buy a few bags of this bud from me." I winked and moved my shoulders to the beat.

"Bud? You got some weed? Word? What you got?"

"I got nickel bags of kush. It's that good smoke too. Straight from Cali. West Side, Loc. You feel me?" I slid a bag out of my pouch and handed it to him.

He stuck his nose to the bag and sucked in the weed's aroma. "Yooooooo, this right here is decent." He looked at one of his boys, who was diggin' through his record crates. "Yo, smell that." He handed him the weed.

"Oh, I got to hit this," his boy said.

I stepped up and said, "I got five-dollar bags. How much you need?"

The deejay handed me forty dollars and I gave them eight bags of weed.

"I tell you what," the deejay said. "They call me Cuddy and I'm always giving a party. And if you give me a percentage, then I'll keep you in business and make sure you're at er' party that I throw. You think you can handle that?"

"Heck yeah."

"Bet."

"A'ight, I'll get up witchu." I wrote my beeper number down on a piece of paper and handed it to him. He winked and said, "I see you, ma."

I waved bye and worked my way over to the B-Boy side. And after I sold them a few bags, I headed for the basketball court, where I completely sold out.

I looked at my beeper and I just knew my eyes were playing tricks on me. I'd sold all of my weed in three hours flat.

Right about now, I didn't care who was looking, I straight broke out into the Pac-Man and just about moonwalked to my car.

I did everything I could to wipe the smile off of my face, so that I could walk in the apartment looking somber.

Get it together.

Stop grinning.

Deep breath.

Now walk in.

I opened the apartment door, and Fresh was sitting on the couch with one of his boys, Saladeen.

Sal nodded.

"Wassup," I said, flat, trying to be extra careful so my voice didn't elevate.

"You good, baby?" Fresh asked. "You back awfully soon. You a'ight?"

"Yeah, I'm good." I pulled a wad of money from my pouch and slid it in his hand. "Half for your payment and the other half for me to re-up. And I'ma need a half a pound this time."

Fresh smiled, the hardest I'd ever seen. "I see your work."

I leaned in and gave him a kiss. "Told you I had this."

35

The weed commandments

After two weeks of killin' it at the park and at Cuddy's parties, I'd made over five thousand dollars. Fresh was straight lovin' my contribution to what he called the family business. And I had to admit, I was feelin' it myself. And although Fresh always kept me fly, I was on my way to kicking things up a notch, from fly to fabulous.

Fresh told me I was making too much money not to have a gun on me. So I carried a little pearl-handle twenty-two in my high-top and I also went back to tucking a blade along the side of my cheek. There were even some nights, when I was pulling in so much money that I had to hire a bodyguard to travel with me. Which was part of the reason Fresh put the word out that I was his girl so everybody on the streets would know who I hustling with.

Hell, we were the Bonnie and Clyde of this thing here, and I planned to keep it that way.

"You ready for school today, baby?" He pulled me in for a kiss as I set his breakfast plate of pancakes and bacon in front of him.

"Yeah, I'm stupid hyped!" I said, now packing three lunch boxes with four jars of peanut butter, each stuffed with a sandwich baggie filled with nickel bags of weed.

"You taking all that to school?"

"Yup."

"And you sure about your crew?" he asked.

"Yeah." I nodded. "Cali and Munch are the two most loyal chicks I know. They my homies. Like family."

"Make sho'."

"They good."

"A'ight. And make sure you run down the rules. If either one of them hesitate or question you, dead it. And tell 'em up front they can't hustle with you. It's a'ight to be cool with your crew, but you gotta let 'em know at all times, that you're in charge. And that's bottom line."

"Fresh, baby." I slung two backpacks over my shoulder. "I got this. Now let me get it."

I hopped in the Chevette and drove over to Da Bricks to pick up Cali and Munch. I'd already called their house last night and told 'em I was picking them up so hopefully they would be outside waiting for me.

When I pulled up, the first person I saw was Yvette. She didn't notice me though. She walked up to one of the dope boys. They exchanged a loaded fist bump, and she quickly rushed back into the building.

"You gon' open the door or what?" Cali said, as she knocked on the car window.

I hit the automatic locks and let them in. "Y'all see Yvette?" I asked.

"I did," Munch said.

"She don't even speak to me no more," Cali said. "She got some new chicks she hang with now."

"I just saw her cop," I said, doing my all to swallow the sting that came along with saying that.

"Yeah, she be out here all the time," Munch said, and we all fell into an awkward moment of silence.

"Enough of that," Cali insisted. "Now let's talk about this money you called us about last night."

"I don't even know what it is and I'm all in." Munch popped her lips.

I started the car and took off up the street. "A'ight, dig. First of all understand that in order to do this you gotta be true to this."

"I hope you not talking about boosting," Cali said. "'Cause Yvette was the only one who could pull that off. I can't do that. I ain't cut out for going to jail, and especially behind no underwear. No, ma'am."

"Would you be quiet?" I said, stopping at a red light. "Ain't noooooobody up in here tryna boost. With the money we can make, we can buy our own gear."

"So get to it. What we gotta do?" Munch asked.

"I'm 'bout to take y'all to the next level," I said.

"How?" they asked simultaneously.

"Hustle. Sell weed." The light changed to green.

They both froze and looked at me strangely. "You serious?" Cali asked.

"Yeah."

"Where we gon' post up at?" Munch asked. "You already know truancy will be stalkin' us if we missin' school to be on the block."

I smiled. "Don't even sweat that. We not gon' be on the block. We gon' bring the block to us. We gon' hustle right here in school." I pulled into the parking lot.

"In school?" Cali looked amazed. "Yo, for real?"

"Heck yeah," I said. "This spot here is a whoooooooole untapped market and we 'bout to seize it."

"Who we sellin' for?"

A smile lit up my face. "Ourselves."

"Not Fresh?"

"Nope. He's just the connect."

"So when we gon' start?" Munch asked, hyped.

"Right now." I reached for my backpack and handed them each a lunch box.

"What's this?" Cali opened the container. "Peanut butter. I 'on't eat no peanut butter! Oh, I thought we was better than this."

"Cali."

"What?"

"Shut. Up, and listen. Now. Inside those jars, after you scoop the first few spoonfuls of peanut butter off the top is a sandwich bag filled with nickel bags of weed."

"Oh, hell yeah! This is crazeeeeee!" Munch said, excited.

"Now listen, this is how we gon' do this. We gon' all take a floor. It's only three floors in the school and it's three of us. Whatever floor your homeroom is on, that's your floor. So I got one. Munch, you got?"

"Three."

I looked over at Cali. "And you got?"

"Two."

"So we only sell weed on our assigned floor?" Munch asked.

"Yep." I nodded. "We gon' run this just like the block and each floor is your corner. You got your corner and I got mine. Now, I want you to give one bag, only. A sample bag, to the biggest weed heads y'all know. That's gon' build up our clientele and I guarantee by this afternoon—"

"We gon' have this whole school on lock," Cali inter-jected.

"And you know it!" I gave her a high five. "Now, it's some rules to this."

"Rules?" Cali frowned.

"Rules," I said. "Er'body got rules, Catherine. So let me break it down. Rule number one: Don't be braggin' 'bout the dough you make. 'Cause it only takes one broke and jealous ho to call five-oh and then we got a problem."

I looked at Munch and Cali, and they both nodded.

I continued, "Rule number two: No credit. If they ask, walk away and tell 'em to come back another day. Rule number three: Don't take no work to class. Period. All work stays in your locker, in the peanut butter jars."

"How we gon' do that?"

"First you get the cash. Then you go to yo' stash. Meet them somewhere safe to make the pass. And walk away from 'em."

"Rule number four is the most important rule of all: Have my money. Period. All of it. Fresh is my man, but this weed ain't free and he wants his cut up front. Now we all family and we all gotta eat. But. I will beat you like a ho in the street if my dough needs Columbo. Feel me?"

They laughed.

"I'm serious."

"A'ight." They nodded. "We got you."

A smile lit up my face. "Now, let's go get paid!"

36

Here, and now, and then

Six months later

Back to life...back to reality... boomed through my hot-pink baby Benz's system, as I rolled up in front of Da Bricks to scoop my crew.

For the last six months, we'd been living life like something outta a movie. We was gettin' money hand over fist.

Throwin' parties.

Hanging out at all the clubs. Mph, with the money we was makin', age was no longer a factor.

We'd even became cool with some rappers and were gettin' backstage passes on the regular.

And gear? Psst. Please.

We had a tailor.

Rocked Chanel bags.

Louie V.

MCM.

Furs in every color.

Fresh kicks for every day of the week, six-inch heels for the weekend.

And not only that, we had a sweet, sweet stash not just in one safe, but in two safes for each of us.

The only thing that I had that Munch and Cali didn't was a car, and that's because they didn't know how to drive. Within a few weeks, we'd be changing all of that.

Me and my girls was making moves all over Newark. Not only was we hustling in school, but we branched out to the basketball and the football games. We served at all of Cuddy's parties.

Fresh was super proud of me, and all he'd say was, "Damn, baby, you in the game now."

"Isis, what, you don't know me no more?" I looked up and Yvette was leaning against the passenger side of the car, looking at me through the window. She was a hundred pounds, at most. Her collarbone stuck out and her eyes seemed to sink into her cheeks. She had an odor and her too-big clothes looked like she'd been wearing them for the last week.

I sucked my teeth. "No, I don't know you. All I know is your name. The chick that I used to know died in a pipe dream."

"No, it ain't like that. I'm clean. I'll admit that I went through some things, but I've changed. I'm clean. I ain't with Flip no more. You was right about him. He ain't nothin'. I shouldn't have ever let him come between us. We family, right?"

"You mean family friends."

"Okay...okay. Maybe I deserve that. But, umm, this what I wanna know. I wanna know if you'll let me get down with you and Cali and Munch." She looked up at them and smiled, and that's when I noticed that they were at the car. She took a step back and let them get in.

"Y'all gettin' money, looking good, and I just wanna be a part of it. That's it."

"What? You better get outta here with that. Go sit down somewhere. When I came to you, before I went to any-body else, you cussed me out and told me no. You said you had your hustle. Boosting. Now go boost and be up outta my face. We got this and no, you can't get it."

"To hell wit' you, Isis! You always thought you was better than somebody! Always thought somebody needed you!"

"You needed me. And I used to need you. We was all we had. But now you out there in the streets with a monkey on your back and you think I'ma put you down. Hell no!" Tears filled my eyes and I quickly wiped them away. "Know what, you better back up and move out my way or I'ma run you over!"

37

Flavor of the nonbelievers

B^{*rgggggggggg!*} *The late bell.*

Dang.

We'd all missed homeroom because of that stupid Yvette. I swear, already she was messing with my money. And now I had to deal with this witch, my history teacher, Ms. Costen. This was the one class that I tried not to say too much in. Mostly because I hated this tramp and didn't ever wanna cuss her out. 'Cause cussin' her out meant suspension. And suspension meant my money for the week would be short.

Not an option.

I eased into the last desk at the back of the classroom. Ms. Costen turned around, as if she had eyes in the back of her head and had seen me come in. "Isis. Did you intend to come to class or was your plan to lollygag in the hallway?"

I sucked my teeth.

Let this go. Just let it go.

I opened my textbook to the chapter she had written on the board, crossed my legs, and then looked at this heifer like she was sick.

"I asked you a question," she pressed, not knowing that she needed to leave well enough alone. I'd already had enough, thanks to Yvette. And I for sure wasn't in the mood for this.

She continued, "Answer me."

"Would you just teach your class?"

Most of the class laughed.

Ms. Costen shook her head. "Quiet." She looked around the class and then turned back to me. "You need to learn some respect. Sitting up in here with these expensive bags, draped in jewels. I don't know how long you think that's going to last with no education. These drug dealers will not take care of you forever."

"Know what? If you keep talking, I'ma haul off and smack the crap outta you! You don't know what you talkin' about and I for sure don't know who you talkin' to. So what you better do is learn to leave well enough alone." I slammed my book closed. "I don't have to take this!" I raised up outta my seat and stormed out of the classroom. I already knew that this whore was gon' call security and then call the office to have me suspended, but whatever. I'd just head to my locker, get my stash and serve my customers at the end of the day.

"Isis Carter," came from behind me. I stopped in my tracks and shook my head. I knew it was security. I didn't even turn around. "I'm going to my locker to get my things and then I'm out. No need to escort me."

"Isis Carter. Stop and place your hands behind your back."

"What?" I whipped around and there were at least five cops behind me. I started to run, but when I looked toward the stairs, there were more cops standing there.

My heart dropped to my feet as two cops walked up on me. One of them placed my hands behind my back and said, "You're under arrest. You have the right to remain silent...."

38

U don't hear me tho

Anything you say can and will be used against you.... I sat in the police station, cuffed to a metal table, across from two pigs who clearly thought they had the nice-cop/pissed-cop routine down to a science. "You may as well tell us the truth." Officer Nice smiled as he leaned forward in his chair, and his partner stood against the wall and ice grilled me. "I like you."

I sucked my teeth. "Yeah, I'm sure you like er'body you arrest."

"Not everybody. But I like you. But Detective Johnson over here, not so much."

"I don't like him either, so we even. And you." I twisted my lips. "I don't even know yo' corny ass and you definitely don't know me."

"I know enough to know you're a good kid. Just made some bad decisions. Your father started a new family and your mother walked off, leaving you pretty much alone. You live with your grandmother, but she's never really

wanted to be bothered with you. And you never really had
any guidance, which is why we're here."

Silence.

He continued, "And all of that is why I wanna help you."

More silence.

"But first, I need you to help me."

I looked the narc dead in the eyes. "I don't care what
you need. You could need air to breathe and I wouldn't
even blow on you."

"Do you realize the trouble you're in?" His voice became elevated, stern, and judging by how red his knuckles
were when he gripped the edge of the table, he was a few
questions away from me getting completely under his
skin.

I shrugged and Officer Pissed jumped in. "Listen. My
partner has the patience of Job. I don't. All I know is that
your little friends are talking, especially the little white
one. She's putting it all on you. And who do you think the
judge is going to believe? So I suggest you cut the crap and
give us some answers."

"You just said my friends was talking. Seems to me if
y'all asked the right questions, then they've already given
you the answers you need. So what you sweatin' me for?
You gon' send me to juvie or not?"

Pissed Off continued, "We were told this was your oper-
ation. Told that you got the drugs from your boyfriend." He
looked over at his partner. "I believe Fresh is his name."

I laughed. Smirked. Slyly bit the inside of my jaw and
prayed the cops didn't hear my heart drop. "Is that the
best you got? You been watching too much TV. What is
this? A *21 Jump Street* routine? Psst, please. Ain't nobody
told you that 'cause I don't even have a boyfriend."

"I believe Rahjohn Bowman is his name, but the streets call him Fresh." They slapped a few surveillance pictures on the table. One of Fresh getting out of his car, with some chick looking over at him. One of him talking to his connect. And another one of him talking to one of his runners. "Look familiar?"

I cross my legs. "Never seen him in my life."

The cop pounded the edge of the table and thrust his face into mine. "I have enough on you to send you away until you're twenty-one. Is that what you want? 'Cause I can make it happen! Now I suggest you get your act together, stop screwing with me, and answer my questions!"

"I don't have to answer nothing. Not a thing. 'Cause I'm only sixteen and y'all know y'all are dead wrong for questioning me without parental consent or my attorney present."

Both of their faces turned beet red.

"Yeah. Exactly. Now I need to make a phone call."

Officer Nice grimaced at me. "I don't care what you need. You could need air and I wouldn't even blow on you."

I sat handcuffed for three hours before Officer Nice stopped violatin' my rights and reluctantly let me make a phone call. "You got two minutes." He handed me the phone and stared in my face.

I sucked my teeth. "God-lee! Can I breathe?!"

He didn't move.

I nixed him and beeped Fresh, **five-oh. nine-one-one.**

Then took a chance and called the brick phone he used for emergencies only.

No answer.

I stared off into space. I didn't know what to do.

"Hang up." Officer Nice frowned. "Time for court."

* * *

"All rise."

Instead of Fresh, Nana's pissed-off face was the first one I saw when the COs escorted me into the courtroom, handcuffed and shackled.

Where is he?

I sucked in my stomach and prayed the nervous tremors in my belly would fade away.

"Raise your right hand," the bailiff barked.

My hand barely inched into the air.

"Do you swear or affirm to tell the truth, the whole truth, and nothing but the truth so help you God?"

"I swear."

"State your name for the record."

"Isis Carter."

"Do you have counsel?"

"Right here, Your Honor." A disheveled and bald white man in a brown polyester suit stepped forward, slamming his briefcase on the table. "My apologies to the court for being late." I breathed a sigh of relief. I knew Fresh wouldn't play me. *Thank you, Jesus.* I tried my best not to let the smile I felt inching across my lips make an appearance. I needed to stay stone faced until they released me.

The judge said, "Counsel, state your appearance."

"Lawrence Cooper. Public defender."

I sucked in a breath. A what? Public defender? Where was my private attorney? Er'body knew that a public defender, better known as a public pretender, meant you would definitely be doing a stint. I swallowed. Held back tears. And did my best to hold it together.

"Counsel." The judge peered over the rim of his glasses. "Your client is charged with resisting arrest and possession with intent to distribute. What does she wish to plead?"

The public pretender leaned over and whispered to me, "Plead guilty. The prosecutor just told me that he's willing to offer a light sentencing. Little jail time and probation, as long as you give up your boyfriend."

If I wasn't handcuffed I'd take it straight to his pale face. "I didn't do anything!" I said, loud enough for the judge to hear.

The public pretender shook his head, looked toward the judge, and sighed in disgust. "Not guilty."

"Okay. The plea has been noted. Another court date will be set. But for now, counsel, whose custody will your client be turned over to?"

Esquire Triflin' looked back at Nana, who was dressed in her short and curly Evangelist wig, with the lace Holy Ghost doily pinned at the scalp. She also had a white ruffled blouse, a blue pleated skirt, white nursing shoes, and a Bible.

I held my head down. Judging by the way she cleared her throat, wasn't no tellin' what was gon' come out of her mouth.

Public Pretender continued, "This is my client's grandmother, Darleen Carter. And she would like to address the court."

Nana was sworn in and then given permission to speak. She popped her lips and proceeded with her madness. "First of all, she ain't comin' to my house! I'm only fifty-three. I need to live my life, not take care of some ungrateful skank who ain't gon' never be nothin'. She don't listen. She fight er' day. And not too long ago, she beat my daughter, her aunt, in the face with a beer bottle. Blood was er'where. Isis does what she wants. When she wants. And how she wants. Hell, I ain't seen her in six months.

So, I wouldn't be surprised if she was selling drugs and usin' 'em. I can't deal with that. I got other grandkids and a great-grandbaby to see about, and I can't be bothered with her anymore. She just a bad seed and all I can do is pray that God is kind enough to have mercy on her devil-ish soul."

"Where are her parents?" the judge asked.

"Her father's in Baltimore. He don't have nothin' to do with her and her mother's a whore, livin' in the streets somewhere. If she ain't dead yet."

"That's enough, ma'am. Take your seat." The judge banged his gavel. He shot me a dirty look. "Remanded until the next court hearing."

39

Keep it underground

"Shoes. Sneakers. Laces. Shirts. Pants. Belts. Bras. Panties. Off. Front and center!"

I couldn't believe this was happenin' to me. I was locked up and standin' in an assembly line of five naked girls: one girl who laughed. One who was dope sick and couldn't stop snot from running over her lips or her teeth from chatterin'. Cali, who was just as pissed off as me, and Munch, who wouldn't stop crying.

There was five COs, all gawkin' and shootin' twisted and sly grins at us.

"Open up!" The correction officers practically shoved a flashlight down our throats as they checked the roofs of our mouths, inner cheeks, and underneath our tongues. Afterwards, they each put on latex gloves and slid their hands down our arms, underneath to our armpits, and under our breasts.

"Now squat. Spread 'em and cough! Now cough again. And again." They walked behind us to see if we farted out any contraband. The girl who was laughing did. Now she wasn't laughing anymore. Immediately they swarmed down on her and then snatched her outta the room, leaving the echo of her screams behind.

"Stand up," the lead CO barked. "Backs straight. Hands to the side. And heads up." He paused. Rushed over to Dope Sick, who was droolin' and shiverin'. "I said stand up!"

Instead, she threw up and fell down in it. He stepped over her and continued, "Hear me and hear me well, I'm not yo' worthless daddies or yo' no-good mamas. I don't care nothin' about you. This is my house. And you will do what I tell you to do. And if you don't, there will be hell to pay.

"Now here are the rules: no cussin'. No contraband. No stealing. Respect the guards. Stay on your pod. No fighting. And mind your business. You got a problem with your cellmates, deal with it. 'Cause I don't wanna hear it." He tossed us each new underwear, orange jumpsuits, socks, and brown rubber slides. "Now go shower and get dressed. You'll be shown your bunks and then you need to report to mess hall."

"Fresh meat! Ohhhh, I like that one right there! Hey yo, ain't that Whatshaname?" serenaded us as we walked single file through the crowded pod, to our dorm of three bunk beds and a steel toilet attached to a sink. We each claimed our bunks in peace, and a few minutes later we were escorted to mess hall.

I felt like I was in the school cafeteria, except there were guards at every corner of the room and everyone had on the same jumpsuit.

Munch was so upset that she stood behind us in the food line, with her arms folded, not saying a word, while

Cali brushed up against my shoulder and I whispered next to her ear, "Word is bond, Yvette dropped dime on us."

"Yvette? What? That's what you think?"

"Yo, that's what I know. Mighty funny how the day I cuss her out is the day we get locked up. She did it."

"But when I see her, I'ma drag her. I promise you that. And I don't care where she's at. On the corner with a pipe in her hand or behind the Dumpster with a trick in her mouth. Wherever I see her, I'm draggin' her out and I'ma stomp her until her rib cage gives way."

The girl in front of me turned around and smiled. "Wassup, Isis?" she asked.

"Wassup?" I said, recognizing her as a chick who lived in Da Bricks.

"What you in here for? Heard you had the whole school slangin'."

My eyes inched over her from head to toe. Her skin was ashy and dry flakes lined her mouth. She was fifty pounds skinnier than the last time I saw her. Her hair was patchy and matted. Her neck had old and new burn marks, like she'd dropped the pipe and the butane lighter one too many times.

A chickenhead.

And I didn't do chicken.

I sold weed. And I sold it in school. Clearly this heifer didn't go to school.

I thought about laying a bolo right in her face. Up here kickin' it to me like we was everyday homegirls when obviously, she was settin' me up. Pressin' me for info today, so the DA could use her to testify against me tomorrow.

I shrugged and said, "I don't sling..." My voice drifted as I spotted Aiesha, the girl whose face I'd sliced, coming toward me.

My heart raced and heated blood rushed to my face. "Cali," I mumbled. "See the girl coming over here toward us?"

"Yeah."

"Well, when I was ten, I sliced her face for trying to rob me." We each eyed Aiesha as she picked up a metal tray. "I think I might have to kill her today."

"Well, I guess we both goin' down together then."

"Isis." Aiesha stepped up to me. "What, you thought I wasn't gon' ever see you again?"

"I wasn't in hiding so I never thought about whether you was gon' ever see me again or not. But now that I've seen you, you can go sit down."

"You don't tell me what to do! I don't have to sit down 'cause you said so!"

"You better back up," Cali said sternly. "I know that much."

I could tell Aiesha didn't know exactly what to say or do. She looked around and made eye contact with a few girls she obviously knew. Their eyes grew wide and they snickered. Obviously, they'd been talking about me.

Cali picked up her carton of milk, shook it, opened it, and, after she took her first sip, twisted her lips. "Girl, this trick ain't stupid. Let's go sit down."

Whap!

My head jerked back, causing me to stumble as Aiesha smacked me across my face. Angry tears beat against the backs of my eyes. I felt like I was back on the playground.

You let some hos disrespect you!

I snatched my steel lunch tray and busted her in the face with it. Blood squirted from her nose and flew everywhere. She fell to the floor and me and Cali started stomping her. Then I yanked her by the hair and sailed a round of punches into her face. Just as I was about to send her through the floor, the guards pepper-sprayed the three of us and snatched us apart. My entire face felt like it was on fire.

The guards handcuffed and shackled us and dragged us down the hall in different directions. And a few seconds later, they tossed me in a small and dark room...where all I could do was cry and pray that Nana's God had enough mercy to kill me by morning.

40

Changes

Nine days.
No TV.
No pen.
No paper.
No yard time.
Nobody to talk to.
Showers er' other day.
And the only way I could tell time was by what was on the food trays they pushed through the door slot.
I just wanted out.
And I put that on everything. I couldn't take it in here no more.
I lay back on the thin blue striped mattress, the hard concrete pushing into my back from beneath.
All I could do in here was think.
Wonder.
What if...I was rich?
Born in the suburbs?

What if my daddy pimped trucks instead of tricks?

What if he was like Cliff Huxtable?

I smiled.

Mike Brady?

My smile grew even wider.

What if Face had never gone to jail?

Schooly never died?

Queenie never left?

Yvette never snitched?

Tears filled my eyes.

Screw what-ifs...what if ain't never did nothing for me but piss me off.

"Ahhhhhhhhhhhhhhhhhhhhh!" I thought about bangin' my head on the wall. Then I remembered they was padded, which pissed me off even more.

The door rattled.

I sat up.

Somebody shoved a letter addressed from Ke'Ron Green and a food tray through the slot: watery eggs, buttered toast, applesauce, and milk.

It was morning.

41

Wild Wild West

Three months later

The CO escorted me out of the bullpen and into the courtroom, handcuffed and shackled. Ready to deal with whatever this public pretender tossed my way. I'd already made up my mind that, lawyer or no lawyer, he had one time to say somethin' slick and he was gon' get cussed out today. I'd had enough of this and all I really wanted to do was get outta here.

I could barely walk, and with all these metal chains and steel garbage on me like I was some kind of criminal, I was forced to take short steps and sway.

The public pretender sat at the defense table, frowning like he clearly couldn't be bothered. I sat down beside him, hands behind my back. He leaned over and said, "Here's the deal. The prosecutor has offered you a plea. Three years' probation. You need to take it. It's only on your juvenile record so when you turn eighteen, it's wiped clean. And another thing, your mother is here to take custody of you—"

My heart dropped. "What?"

He continued on like he hadn't heard me stop breathing or my heart hitting the floor. "Yes. She's outside the courtroom. The sheriff's deputy will bring her in at any moment. The plan is for her to take you home."

"What?"

"You are to be quiet until I tell you to address the court. Don't grunt. Don't groan. Say, 'yes, Your Honor,' and if the judge asks you about some animalistic fight you apparently got into, you are to apologize. As a matter of fact, even if the judge doesn't mention it, you apologize anyway. You say you are committed to being a better person. And that you will never find yourself in another situation like this again. Now you either say that or you find yourself sent back to jail until your trial is over. Understand?"

"All rise," the bailiff said before I could respond.

The judge took the bench. "Good morning. Counsel, please state your appearance for the record."

"Claire Wallace. State's prosecutor."

"Lawrence Cooper. Representing the defendant."

I heard the courtroom double doors squeak open. And I could hear people walking in, but there was no way I could turn around to see who they were. Then I felt a hand lay on my shoulder and squeeze.

I wanted to scream, "Get offa me!" But I didn't. I sat there. Like stone. Hearing the judge and the lawyers speak but not really knowin' what they was sayin'.

All I knew is that it had been three years, five months, two weeks, and an afternoon that Queenie had been gone. And then just like that she wanted to show up like it was all good in the hood.

I don't think so.

I knew I needed to be quiet long enough to get outta here, then I could cuss Queenie out.

I tried to swallow the iron fist I felt balling up in my throat. I failed.

"My client would like to address the court," the public pretender said, giving me a loaded glare like he dared me to flip the script.

I struggled to stand up. "Your Honor." I paused. Pushed the cusses and the "forget all of y'alls" that I really wanted to say back down into my throat and said, "I would like to apologize to the court for my behavior. And I will not place myself in a situation like this again."

The judge looked over his glasses. "I certainly hope not, young lady. Because the next time I will make you a ward of the court."

"Your Honor," my attorney said. "My client is willing to accept the plea. Also, her mother is here and she would like Isis to be released to her custody."

"I thought the mother was missing, as the grandmother stated at the last hearing."

"Your Honor, there appeared to be some kind of mistake."

Mistake? Yeah, right.

"The mother lives in Atlanta now, and she's promised to make sure my client is brought back and forth to court."

Atlanta!

I did everything I could to keep myself together.

Just chill.

You almost outta here.

The same hand that squeezed my shoulder before, squeezed it again. I knew for a fact that it had to be Queenie. I didn't turn around, though, because I knew if I did, it was no tellin' what I would say or what I would do. So I looked straight ahead at the judge, whose eyes combed my file. "The court will release Miss Carter into her mother's custody." He looked up. "Court in a month." He banged his gavel. "Dismissed."

The processing officer handed Queenie my paperwork and then looked at me and wished me luck. I felt like I was about to burst into scorchin' flames.

I couldn't even look this trick in the face. I glanced at Queenie once and then quickly looked the other way. I couldn't believe she was standing here. Like she hadn't walked out and left me with the devil.

Once we were outside and I was free and clear of the court and the COs, I looked up at Queenie, fought back angry tears, and said, "You may as well carry yo' behind back to the track you just left 'cause I ain't goin' nowhere with you!"

"Don't you dare speak to me like that! I'm your—"

"My what? My mother? I know you was not about to say that! 'Cause last I checked, it's been exactly three years and an afternoon since we got down as anything, let alone as mother and daughter."

"Isis. I can explain, but I need you to calm down."

"You need me to calm down? Really? Screw you! Where were you when I needed you? Huh? Where were you? Off on some bus somewhere rollin' to Atlanta. Did you forget you had a daughter?"

"How could I forget something like that?"

"You tell me, 'cause after Schooly died you didn't care nothing about me! You just left me by myself." Tears were flying everywhere. "I swear to God, I hate you! I hate you! And if you think I'm going anywhere with you, then you are dead-ass wrong!" And I stormed away, leaving her in the middle of the block with tears covering her face.

42

Protect ya neck

No money.
No beeper.
No phone.
Feet on fire.
Head about to explode.

I'd stormed through countless Newark blocks, from the courthouse to Fresh's apartment, only to find him smoking a blunt with two gigglin' tricks.

Wham! Bam! Pow! With everything in me, I hooked off and one-twoed him right in his face. Painful surprise caught him and he stumbled back. I kicked him in his chest and just as I went to follow up with another round of spontaneous kicks and punches, he wrapped a hand around my neck and slammed me into the wall.

"You must want me to shoot you!" He tightened his grip on my throat. "What the hell is wrong witchu?" He flung me from the wall to the couch.

He looked over at the two chicks, who were no longer giggling. "Y'all need to leave. Now!"

"For what? They been chillin' here witchu, so why they gotta leave now?" I looked over at the chicks, who were walking toward the door. "No, y'all stay."

Fresh shot them a look and they rushed out the door, as I shoved him in his chest.

I screamed, "Where have you been, huh? What happened to my lawyer? Money for my account?! A goddamn visit?!"

"A visit? And why would I come up there? You of all people should already know that the last place I'm gon' be is visiting you in jail!"

"You could've sent a lawyer!"

"You're a minor. You didn't need a big-time lawyer. I knew you would get off!"

"I had to take a plea for probation. You think that's getting off? Are you serious?"

"You need to be grateful!"

"Really? Grateful? So that's why you didn't do anything for me, not even send me money, because I should be grateful!"

"Money? You know how dry it's been for me around here? And who was I gon' send the money by? Your crackhead cousin, who's strung out and selling five-dollar blow jobs on the street!"

I felt like he'd just stuck me with a knife full of salt in my chest. "You know what? I went to jail, and the only person who cared enough about me to see how I was doin' was K-Rock. And he said some things that made a lot of sense."

"So he tells you what to do now?"

"It's not about him telling me what to do. It's about me knowing when to take some advice. So hear me when I say this: I'm done selling weed. Finished!"

"What?"

"You heard me. So don't even look at me to hustle any-more."

"Oh." He arched a brow. "Word? And what you gon' do? Work at McDonald's? Burger King? Is that how you wanna repay me, after er'thing I've done for you?"

"Listen. It's no crew. They're done too. We all got a lil stash. Er'body trying to change their ways, finish school. Maybe go to college."

"College? What? Here's what you need to do. Get outta this fairy tale you in and K-Rock needs to stop puttin' bull-shit in your head. 'Cause you don't have no skills. You pretty, but you don't have no talent, so I don't know how long you think them looks gon' last."

"First of all, I'ma hustler and I'ma always make a way to survive! I been on my own ever since my brother died, so I don't need you!"

"Look, hold on, you got me messed up. You the one who wanted to come into this marijuana game. I ain't even know you had the heart for it until you showed me what you was capable of. And er'body in the streets know that if it wasn't for your crackhead cousin runnin' her mouth, you would still be slangin'."

"Do you understand that I just got outta jail? And I had to take a plea for probation. One screw-up and I'm back in jail. I'm not interested!"

"Oh, so now you wanna bitch up 'cause you got locked up. You did three months and suddenly you wanna do a whole one-eighty. I ain't tryna hear that from you. My coke and weed connect is locked up, which means my money is funny. So the last thing I'm tryna hear is you telling me that you about to screw wit' even more of my dough."

"Fresh—"

"So you will sell weed, at school, and you ain't gon' stop until I tell you to." Fresh peered through me as if he dared me to say something else, and when I didn't, he continued with, "Now I got someplace to go. And when I get back you better have your thoughts straight!"

He walked out of the living room and headed to his bedroom, leaving me standing there.

I couldn't believe this was happening to me. I felt dizzy and saw visions of Queenie dancing before me. How could she be back and living in Atlanta? Atlanta? So she just left me here while she ran off and started a whole other life somewhere else... probably with somebody else....

"Isis, you hear me?"

I blinked as Fresh's voice brought me out of my thoughts. I looked him over, my eyes stopping at the gold watch on his arm....

"Lil sis, you still mad at me? I traded one of those gold necklaces for a box of Chick-O-Sticks. So you wouldn't be mad anymore....I'm sorry I told you to eat it. And check it, if you want, and if it means that much to you, I'll take everything off. 'Cept the watch. 'Cause I really like it."

"A'ight, I'll let you rock wit' the watch."

"Fresh, where you get that watch from?"

"My cousin Snoop gave it to me. Why?"

"'Cause my brother had a watch like that."

"Your brother? What's your brother's name?"

"Schooly."

Fresh blinked. His thoughts drifted and then he looked

back over at me. "Schooly? Hold on. Was your brother the lil retarded boy that got killed?"

"Don't call my brother retarded. Now how did you get that watch?"

He curled his upper lip in disgust. "Just answer my question, was your brother the lil retarded boy? Who got killed because his brother Face set up my homeboy?" He paused, his eyes loaded with a million thoughts. "Hold up? Is Face your brother too?!" He snatched my cheeks and squeezed them.

"Get offa me!"

"I asked you a question!"

"Yes, Face is my brother!"

"He killed my cousin, Snoop! And here I been messing with you." He reared his fist back and before I could even attempt to free myself from his grip, all I could feel was his fist landing in my face....Everything around me faded to black.

I opened my eyes and Fresh stood over me, as I lay on the floor. "You lucky that's all you got. Now what you better do is tell me exactly how your brother got this watch. Or I'ma stomp blood from you and I mean that."

Tears flooded my face. I scooted back, gripped the couch, and pulled myself up and off the floor. I sat on the edge, scared of what Fresh might do next. "Look, my brother Face used to sling, but he was also a stick-up artist."

"I know. And he stuck his hand in the wrong goddamn pocket this time. Now keep talking."

"All I know is that my brother and his homeboy—"

"Who, K-Rock?" Fresh placed his hand at his side, where his gun was tucked.

"No! K-Rock is freakin' square. A college boy. He don't

know nothing about these streets. And like I said, my brother and his homeboy—"

"What's his name?"

I shrugged. "I don't know. All I know is that he and Face robbed some drug dealer—"

"Yeah, my cousin Snoop's right-hand man, George, and his crew is who they ran up on."

"Okay, they robbed George and his crew. And they took his money and his jewelry. And when they came home, Face gave Schooly that watch."

"Yeah, and this watch is why Snoop caught your little retarded brother at the bus stop and left him dead under the bridge. Which, as far as I'm concerned, his lil slow ass deserved. I don't believe this!" He slammed his hands against his temples, like his thoughts pained him.

I did everything I could to hold it together. I knew if I yelled, screamed, or made any sudden move that Fresh just might kill me or come close to it. He looked at me with rage and disgust. "Trick! You lucky I ain't know you was Face's little sister or I would've finished his family off, especially after he killed my cousin."

Whap!

The scorching heat of Fresh's slap stunned me as I fell into the wall and hit the back of my head. I spotted the butt of his twenty-two on the end table and immediately my instincts told me to pick it up and shoot this . . .

"Let me tell you somethin'." I snatched the twenty-two and gripped it in my hand. "If you hit me again, I'ma send you visiting, and the same sucker-ass Snoop that you beatin' for gon' be the one you stop by to see!"

Blood dripped from my busted bottom lip and I flung it away. Fresh frowned and took a step closer to me.

I knocked off the safety.

"Put the gun down!" he ordered.

"Back up and you better not hit me again!"

He took another step forward. "What did I just say?!"

"Back. Up."

Fresh rushed over toward me and just as I positioned my finger to squeeze the trigger, he snatched the gun from my hand. "What are you, stupid? I need to be the last person you pull a gun on!"

"Don't touch me again! Or I'ma pull the trigger the next time."

"Then you better make sure the gun is loaded. 'Cause this one is empty."

"Well, then it's your lucky night."

Fresh shook his head and paced the room. He looked over at me and shook his head again. "I don't believe this!" he said as he tossed a punch into the air. Then he turned back toward me and said, "Sit down, Isis."

"I'm not sitting down! Are you crazy?!" I wildly wiped the tears streaming from my eyes.

He shot me a look. "What did I just say? Sit down."

"No!"

Fresh hopped up and walked over to me. I flinched. "Look." He gripped my shoulders. "Had I known you were Face's lil sister, I would've never looked your way. But it's nothing I can do about it. I love you—"

"Puttin' your hands on me is not love!"

"Would you shut up! That's your problem—you're always running your mouth. You need to listen sometimes! It's messed up about what happened to your brother, but Face caused that. You know the rules. You come for me I come even harder for you. Fair exchange no robberies. You know that."

"Schooly never did nothing to anybody! They didn't have to kill him!" I screamed and pushed him in his chest. I was doing everything in my power to stop these tears from burning down my face but, I couldn't.

"Well, you need to blame Face. He did that. And word is bond, you need to be thankful that didn't nobody off you."

I was slowly losing my mind. All I wanted to do was slice Fresh across his throat and make him regret everything he'd just done to me. But I knew there was a time for everything....

Fresh continued, "None of this had to be. But it is."

Silence.

"But I'ma forgive you."

Forgive me?

He carried on. "Only 'cause you really didn't know. And I care about you." He paused. "And I'm sorry about what happened to your brother. But right now, I can't stay stuck on that. I gotta get back on top of my game and we need to get things back on track. And make this money."

Knock! Knock!

Fresh squinted and looked toward the door.

"Isis! You in there? Open up this door!"

Queenie...

"Isis!" She pounded. "You in there? Open this door right now!"

"Who is that?" Fresh reached for his gun.

"You don't need that. It's my mother."

He frowned. "Your what? Your mother?"

"ISIS!" Queenie screamed. "Yvette told me this is where your boyfriend lives! So you better open up this door or I will have the police here!"

Fresh arched a brow. "I tell you what. You better get

that old trick away from my door talking about the police or I'ma raise the body count in a minute."

"You not about to shoot my mother."

"You trying to find out?"

"Isis!"

I stormed over to the door and snatched it open. Queenie pushed her way inside. "Let's go!"

"I ain't goin' nowhere witchu! So you may as well go back wherever you came from and leave me alone. You ain't been worried about me, so why are you all up and in my business now?"

"I don't know who you think you're talking to, but obviously you forgot who I am. Now I made some mistakes, leaving you being one of them. But I'm here and lucky for you, I came back right on time. Otherwise you'd be sitting in some girls' home somewhere...." She paused. "What happened to your face?" She grabbed my face and I flinched away. "Who did this to you?"

"None of your business!"

She walked over to Fresh. "You put your hands on my daughter."

"You better go 'head. I ain't touch your daughter."

"Do you know I will slice your throat?!" she snapped at Fresh. "You put your hands on my daughter!" She took a step closer to him.

I slid in between them. "Queenie, would you stop!" I screamed. "Just go! Just leave! You don't have a right coming up in here like this! You don't tell me what to do! I'm grown!"

"Well, I have custody of your grown ass. Now you decide." She looked over at Fresh. "I don't know who you are, but I know you did this to my daughter. She's a minor.

And right now, I'm telling you, if my daughter doesn't come with me willingly then I will be calling the police to make her go! Now you help her decide."

"The police?" Fresh said, looking over at me. "How about this? Both of y'all got to go."

"Fresh, wait a minute."

"Ain't no wait a minute."

"Fresh—"

"You gotta go!"

"I'm not going anywhere with you!"

"Oh, you goin'," Fresh spat. "I'm not about to deal with this!" He opened the front door. "I care about you and I wish things could've been different, but I'm not about to get locked up behind this."

"Let's go, Isis!" Queenie grabbed me by my wrist, pulled me out the door, and before I could pull away from her, Fresh slammed the door behind me.

I rode quietly in the cab with Queenie, staring out the window. "Sometimes, I feel like I should've died the minute I was born."

"Why would you say something like that?!"

"Then I wouldn't have to go through this. Especially if the people who had me wasn't gon' stick around to take care of me."

"Don't say that." Queenie stroked my hair.

"Get off of me."

"Isis—"

"You and Daddy dumped me in these streets. Just left me like I wasn't nothin'. And then you show up demanding that I come with you, not caring about what I wanted or how I've been living since you left!"

"That's not true. I have missed you. I left because I had to get my thoughts straight. I was in mourning—"

"What?" I turned around and looked at her. "So what? I should feel sorry for you?"

"Isis, I thought I was doing the right thing by walking out and leaving you with your grandmother."

Now she'd pissed me off. "See, this is exactly why I ain't even wanna be bothered with you. How you gon' sit there and say you thought you were doing the right thing? By leaving me? By not even saying good-bye? See you later? Even you saying 'I ain't coming back' would've been better than you turning into air."

"You were a child. I didn't know how to come and talk to you the way that you needed me to. That way that I should've."

"Do you know how many nights I looked for you, and looked for you, and looked for you? Huh? Do you know what it was like living with Nana? She didn't buy us nothing. She didn't talk to us. She cussed us out. She hated us. And you thought you were doing the right thing? The only thing you left me with was a slap across the face. And that lasted for three years and, as far as I'm concerned, you still slapping me."

"Isis." She draped an arm over my shoulders. "I didn't know."

I flung her arm off of me. "You didn't care. You were wrapped up in Queenie. And Schooly. And everything else you lost, instead of looking at me. I was right there. Right there. And it didn't matter to you—"

"It did matter. That's why I didn't take you with me!"

"You didn't take me with you because you didn't see me as being worth it. And now you wanna come back and lay out your new life and tell me I can have a new start, when I ain't never had a start in the first place, I just had to make it."

"Isis, when I got on that bus, I didn't know where I was going. All I knew is that I had to leave and get away from everything. And I was wrong to leave you. I know that now. But I was empty. I need you to understand that. I didn't have nothing. I was a whore, living with a pimp, yo' daddy, and the life we lived was hell. And I was tired of hell. My mother died when I was seven. I never knew my father. My aunt raised me and she didn't wanna do that. So I ran away at fourteen and I met Zeke. I thought he was the answer to everything, but he wasn't."

"So you ran away again and left me here."

"I'm sorry."

"And triflin'." The cab pulled up at a red light. "I'm outta here."

"Isis, I'm not letting you go anywhere!"

"Screw you!" I hopped out of the cab and ran across the street.

Queenie hopped out behind me. "Where are you going?!"

"I don't know 'cause I don't have anywhere to go!" I was trying to hold myself together, but I couldn't. "Do you understand how tired I am? I was selling weed trying to make it on my own. Went to jail! Now I'm out. I don't have nowhere to turn. Nowhere to go! I don't have nothing! Nothing! And now you wanna come and take what little I do have away from me!"

"And what little is that? Your boyfriend? Let me tell you something, I been exactly where you are, and all he is going to do for you is pull you down. And if you think for one minute that he loves you—"

"I know you of all people are not about to lecture me about love. What? You love me? Really? Is that how you love your child, by leaving them? You think I wanna be with Fresh like this? Depending on him? You think I don't want to be away from him?! Do you see what he did to my face?"

Tears streamed down Queenie's face. "Isis, I'm so, so sorry. I am. And I am willing to spend the rest of my life making it up to you. But if you want out, truly, truly want out then I need you to listen to me."

"Listen to you for what?"

"Before you were brought into court today, I had a conversation with the detective. And he came up with a plan."

43

Till infinity

I promised Queenie that I wouldn't run away but told her that I needed her to give me a minute to breathe. At first I wasn't sure where I was going...all I knew was that I needed a minute to myself.

I rang K-Rock's bell and prayed that he answered the door. I wrung my hands and tapped the balls of my sneakers, as I pressed the bell again.

Ding...dong...

A few moments later the knob and the lock jiggled from the other side.

K-Rock. Thank you, Jesus.

He opened the door and said, surprised, "Icy?"

"Yeah."

"Come in." He closed the door behind me. "Wassup? What you doing here?"

"K-Rock, I really need to talk to you."

"Sure, baby. What's going on?" He sat down on the edge of the couch.

My throat swelled with tears, as I slid my glasses off and untied my hood. K-Rock looked into my face and jumped up. He walked over to me and lightly grabbed my cheek. "Yo, what the...what happened to you? And don't tell me nothin' about Yvette, 'cause I'm not gon' believe it."

I shook my head. "Not Yvette. My boyfriend—"

"Your boyfriend? He did this to you? Where he at? 'Cause I'ma handle him today. This gon' be the last time he puts his hands on you."

"No, please. I don't need you to do that. I need you to listen to me."

"I don't need to listen. You've already said enough. He did this to you and now I'm about to go and see about him."

"Would you listen to me?! I need to tell you this!"

"Tell me what?"

"He had on Schooly's watch."

"What?"

"Yes. He came out the bedroom with Schooly's watch on. I confronted him and things got ugly."

"Wait. Hold up. Who's your boyfriend? What's his name?"

"They call him Fresh."

K-Rock looked at me like I was crazy. "You over there chillin' wit' Fresh? Do you know that's Snoop's cousin? Snoop, who killed Schooly. Snoop, who Face killed."

"I know that now! But I didn't know he was anything to Snoop. And he just found out I was Face's sister and he went ballistic on me!"

"You lucky he didn't kill you! You hardheaded! I keep telling you to leave these streets alone, but you don't listen to nobody. You think you know everything. Now I got to go out there and risk my freedom 'cause I'ma have to put a bullet in his head, 'cause if I don't he most definitely gon' put one in yours."

"I don't need you to do that! I need you to just be here for me. Give me a moment to figure things out. I'm messed up right now, Queenie showed up at the courthouse."

"She did what?"

"You heard me. After all this time, she just appears like I'm supposed to run off in the sunset so we can chill. Well, that ain't happening. And you know I can't go back to my grandmother's house."

"You can go back to your grandmother's. You just don't wanna humble yourself and apologize."

"Apologize for what? She put me out!"

"Listen, your grandmother loves you. Otherwise she would've never took you in."

"I'm not going back there. I'm not."

"Well, you can't go back to Fresh's."

"I have to."

"What, you got a death wish? Who do you think you playing with? Do you know how dangerous he is? How much do you even know about this dude? You know he's my age right?"

"Yeah, but he ain't you."

"No, he ain't me, 'cause I would never put my hands on you!"

"Yeah, you would never hit your lil sis." I sucked my teeth. "You know what?" I slid my shades back on. "I got this."

"You got what? You don't have nothin'. That's your problem—you don't never wanna deal with nothin'. I don't know what you tryna be so tough for. You think I don't know you checkin' for me? You know how long I been checkin' for you? But you was too young—"

"And what about now?! Or are you going to keep lying to yourself!"

He walked over to me and pressed his forehead against mine. "No. I'm not going to keep lying to myself. I want you. I do. But I need you to get yourself together. All this selling weed and going to jail. And Fresh. It's too much. I ain't in that life no more."

"But this is all I know."

"Learn something different then."

I stared at K-Rock and looked deeply into his eyes. He was everything I wanted and more. But this wasn't about him. This was about saving my life. "You're right. I need to learn something different. Do something different. But first I got some unfinished business I need to take care of with Fresh."

"And what's that?"

I smiled and brushed him softly with a kiss. "Listen to this..."

44

Criminal minded

Ring...ring...
"Hello."

"Hello. This is Isis Carter. Remember me...?"

"Yes. I sure do."

"Well, remember you said that you needed me? Well, now I need you." I chuckled. "And no. I don't need air to breathe. Okay. Yes. I can meet you in an hour. Thank you." Click.

By the time I got back to Fresh's, he was on the phone yelling about having no connect. I walked into the kitchen and looked him dead in the eyes. Before he could tell me to leave or get pissed off about me being here I placed a duffel bag filled with five pounds of marijuana in front of him.

Fresh hung up the phone without even saying good-bye. "Yo, where you get this from?" he said to me, like he was seeing things.

"I got it from my brother's homeboy."

"Homeboy? What's his name?"

I hesitated. "It's Rick. And he owed me a favor, so I asked him to hook me up with his weed connect and he did."

"What?" He gave me a suspicious smirk.

"Yeah. I got us some weight. And I know things are tough for you right now, so I bought that for you. And if you want, I can introduce you to him, and you two can take things from there."

"And where is your mother?"

"She's not going to bother us. I promise."

"Your brother's homeboy?" He frowned. "I already don't trust him."

"Nah, baby, he's good people. I promise you. He's a friend of the family. K-Rock knows him too. And I know you're in a tight spot, which is why I wanted to check things out and get that for you myself." I pointed to the table. "Hopefully, this'll help us get back on the right track and get past all of the nonsense trying to get in between us."

Fresh didn't say anything. He just stared at me.

"I'm saying, baby, just take the weed and push it. And if you want, I'll set up a meeting, introduce you to him, and you two can take it from there."

He hesitated. "Okay. A'ight. Call him up. 'Cause I'ma need more than five pounds. I'ma need at least ten more. You think he could do that?"

"Yeah, I'm sure. I mean, I just got five from him, so he should be able to do ten."

I picked up the phone and quickly dialed the number. "Johnson, hey, wassup. It's Isis. Can you get back in touch with Nice for me? 'Cause Fresh needs to get a little bit more."

"Okay," Johnson said. "Say no more. Meet me in three

hours at the spot." Click. I looked at Fresh after I hung up and said, "Done."

"A'ight."

Three hours later, as Fresh and I drove to the spot, he smiled and told me about another meeting he had set up for tomorrow for a new coke connect. "That's beautiful, baby." I forced myself to smile.

"I know it's been rough, Isis. But once I get my money rolling in again and my connects in place, baby, we gon' be straight. I promise you that."

"Pull over there," I said, pointing to where Johnson stood in front of a short brick building. "There he is."

Once we were out of the car Fresh tapped the side of his pants and adjusted his gun. Then he slung his duffel bag, filled with money, over his shoulder.

"Johnson, this is Fresh and, Fresh, this is Johnson," I said, as Fresh and I walked over to him.

They gave each other dap. "Oh, so this is Fresh," Johnson said. "A'ight. A'ight. Good to meet you, come on inside." He walked us into a sparsely furnished one-bedroom apartment.

"Appreciate you hooking me up, man," Fresh said. "My connects got locked up and ain't nothin' been right since."

"I understand that," Johnson said.

"The streets been drying up for me and I just need a little something to get me back straight."

"So what you need?"

"You got ten for me?"

"Yeah. Give me a minute." Johnson walked into the back of the apartment and quickly returned with a garbage bag filled with weed.

Fresh's face lit up as he and Johnson made an even exchange.

Johnson placed the duffel bag on the floor, while Fresh looked through the garbage bag and inspected the weed. "A'ight, this is lookin' right."

"I bet it is," Johnson spat. "Now hold your head up and place your hands behind your back."

"What?!" Fresh jerked his head up and Johnson had his gun drawn and pointed at him. Fresh reached for his gun, but before he was able to retrieve it, the room filled with police. "You have the right to remain silent," Detective Johnson said to Fresh.

"You set me up!" Fresh yelled. "I can't believe this, after everything I've done for you! This is what you do!"

"So what you gon' bitch up, 'cause you got locked up? Charge it to the game."

EPILOGUE

Two years later

"I hope you all heard me and took notes." I looked around the room at the small group of troubled youth. "My life wasn't easy. I had to fight for everything I had. And I made some terrible decisions, which is what I don't want you all to do."

"How did you make it? I don't know if I could've survived all of that," one of the girls said.

"I had no choice but to make it work for me. Like my mother once told me, I'm a survivor."

"How's your relationship with your mother now, Isis?"

"It's better. It took some time though. After Fresh was arrested, I moved down here to Atlanta to live with my mother. We had to get to know each other and we're still learning."

A young man raised his hand. "Do you think you're a snitch for what you did? In my hood, you don't run your mouth like that."

"Young man!" one of the counselors admonished.

"No." I smiled. "It's okay. You know what, all that 'don't

snitch, don't tell' is crazy. When your life or somebody else's life is in danger, you have to do what's right. How long do you think I could've lived with Fresh before he killed me? Or tossed me out into the street? Or I was arrested again because of some drugs he had in the house? Not long. I had to do the right thing. For me. And for my brother, Schooly."

"So did you take back the watch?"

"I sure did."

Another young man raised his hand. "So what about your friends?"

"Well, Munch and Cali are both in college, like me. Except they are still in New Jersey."

"Are you still friends?"

"Yes. We're not as close as we used to be, but we still talk and catch up."

"What about K-Rock?"

"I'm still here," K-Rock said from the back of the room. "I'm not going anywhere."

All I could do was blush.

"What about Yvette?" someone shouted from the back of the room.

"Yvette is still out there in the streets. I'm hoping and praying that one day she'll be standing here able to tell her story. I thank you all for listening to me and I truly hope that if nothing else, hearing everything that I've gone through will make a difference."

A READING GROUP GUIDE

DOWN BY LAW

Ni-Ni Simone

ABOUT THIS GUIDE

The following questions are intended to
enhance your group's reading of
DOWN BY LAW.

Discussion Questions

1. *Down By Law* takes place in the 1980s. What do you think would've been different had the story taken place today? What do think would've been the same?

2. What do you think it means to be down by law?

3. The first chapter is titled "The Message." What message do you believe Isis received from her parents? How do you think this message influenced her decisions in life? Do you believe Isis's parents gave her brothers the same message?

4. Face was Isis's oldest brother. What influence do you believe he had over her life? Do you know anyone who has a brother like Face?

5. How do you think Face, K-Rock, and Isis robbing the drug dealers changed their lives forever? In what way?

6. How do you think Isis's life would've been different had Schooly not been killed?

7. What kind of mother do you think Queenie was? Do you think she loved Isis? What do you think of her leaving Isis with Nana? Do you know any mothers like Queenie?

8. What kind of father do you think Zeke was? Do you think he loved Isis? Why do you think he treated her

the way he did when she went to see him on her sixteenth birthday?

9. What did you think of K-Rock? What did you think of
his decision to change his life? What did you think of
his parents?

10. What do you think Yvette's future will be?

Don't Miss
Caught Up
by Amir Abrams

School's out and sixteen-year-old Kennedy Simms is bored. That could be a recipe for disaster...

Available wherever books and ebooks are sold.

Turn the page for an excerpt from *Caught Up*...

1

Swaggerlicious. That's the word that comes to mind to describe this dark-skinned cutie-pie standing in front of me with the gold fronts in his mouth, pierced ears, and an arm covered in intricately designed tattoos trying to get his rap on. Swag plus delicious equals *swaggerlicious*. Not that *that's* a real word found in Webster's dictionary or anything. No. It's found in the hood. It oozes out of the music. It jumps out at you in the videos. It's splattered all over the pages of *Vibe* and *XXL* and every other hip-hop magazine there is. It's flooded in the pages of every urban fiction novel I've coveted over the last two years. It airs on *Love & Hip Hop* and *BET*. Okay, okay, maybe there's more ratchetness than swaggerlicousness on those TV shows. Still...it's there. That hood swag.

And it's my guilty craving. It's my dirty secret.

I want it.

Swag.

I ache to know what it's like to be caught up in the ex-

citement of the fast-paced street life found across the
other side of town—right smack in the heart of the hood,
where I am not ever allowed to be. Where the streets are
hot and alive and full of excitement.

God, my parents would have a full-fledged heart attack
if they knew I was saying this, that I'm attracted to the
hood life. Fascinated and intrigued by it.

See. I'm from the suburbs. Live in a gated community.
And swag doesn't exist here. Not in my eyes. Not in my
opinion. And definitely not in the way it lives and breathes
in the hood. Or in the *ghetto,* as my mom would call it.

But I personally don't think there's anything *ghetto*
about the hood. I think ghetto is a state of mind as well as
a state of being. And I definitely don't think everyone who
lives in the hood is ghetto. But of course, my parents, par-
ticularly my mom, would beg to differ. Whatever.

Anyway, back to my quest for swag. I attend an all-girls
private school. And trust me, swag definitely isn't there, either. Nope. I'm surrounded by girls whose only focuses
are cotillions, prom gowns, graduations, sleepovers, shopping sprees, dating boys with promising futures, while
preparing for the SATs.

Can you say *borrrrrriiiing.*

My life is swagless!

Don't get me wrong. I dress nice. *Cute* is more like it.
Okay, maybe a little preppy. Still, I have nice things. And I
am always nicely dressed nonetheless. However, sometimes
I feel like a fashion loser—even though I *know* it's all in my
head—when I see a clique of girls stylishly dressed in all the
hottest designer labels, strutting through the mall, yapping
it up, catching the eyes of boys with a whole lot of hood
swag.

That's the girl I want to be—the girl with the sexy strut and a whole lot of sass. Not that there's anything wrong with who I am now. It's just that...I mean. I'm a cutie and all. And I have a nice body, from what I'm told. And lots of guys try to talk to me. Still...for the most part, I am a really basic girl. No lipstick. No eyeliner. Not a lot of fuss with my crinkly hair. Not much time spent in the mirror. Basically, I'm what my mother calls "low maintenance."

Translation: Plain Jane. Nothing special. Ordinary looking.

Yup, that's me. Plain ole, ordinary-looking Kennedy, with nothing special going on in her life. Well, guess what? School is out. It's the start of summer. And if I have my way, a change is about to come. Soon.

"So, what's good witchu, ma?" Mr. Swag says, reaching out and touching my left cheek. He's about five-ten with a slim but muscular build. He kind of reminds me of a sprinter. Lean and trim. "You real sexy, babe."

I smile. "Thanks."

"You make me wanna do some thangs to you; real spit, ma. Who you out here wit'? I been checkin' for you for a minute."

I blush. Tell him I'm here with my friend Jordan. This is like the fourth time I've *run* into him at the mall. The first time was a few weeks back. He was with a crew of guys all dressed in different color POLO sweat suits with matching snapback hats and limited-edition Nikes. They were all looking like they should be on the cover of the latest *Hip Hop* magazine. And when he called me over to him, I felt my nervousness give way to excitement, like right now.

"Oh word? That's wassup. So how 'bout you 'n' me go grab a bite to eat real quick so we can get better acquainted while ya peeps do what they do?"

I glance at my watch. "I can't. I have to find my friend then get ready to go." It's a bold-faced lie. Truth is, I don't date much. I mean, I do. But I only date guys who are parent-approved. And this fine boy right here is definitely, unequivocally, not someone my parents would ever allow me to go off anywhere with, let alone date—even if it is only up to the next level of the mall to get something to eat. Not that it's a date. Not that he's even asking me out on one or anything like that. Although I wish like heck he would. Then again, maybe I don't.

I eye the thick chain hanging from his neck, wondering if it's silver, stainless steel, or white gold and if the diamonds in the cross dangling from it are real. My gaze shifts down to his half-laced Timberlands, then back up. I swallow. My mouth waters at the way his sagging jeans hang off his narrow hips, showing the waistband of his POLO boxers. He has on a Gucci belt.

Swaggerlicious. Hmmm. Yes, that's him. The expression used to describe someone who has lots of swag and loads of confidence. It's in the way someone walks, and talks, and carries himself. And it's a word I would never, ever, be caught dead using in front of my besties—or worse, my parents.

They'd die.

No scratch that. They'd kill *me* first. Then die.

How dare I want to use such street slang? How dare I want to toss away thousands and thousands of dollars' worth of my parents' hard-earned money they've spent to send me to the best private schools in order to shield me from such atrocities. I'd be damned to hell for eternity, roasting a hundred deaths, for shaming them.

Okay, okay. I'm being facetious.

I'm overexaggerating; just a little.

Still…they'd probably want to lock me away until my twenty-first birthday if they even thought I was standing here contemplating ditching my bestie to go off with this guy who I've only been talking to for—I glance at my watch—seventeen minutes and thirty-six seconds. He could be a stalker. Or worse.

A hoodlum.

A thug.

I want to laugh at the absurdity.

Rule number one: No hoodlums allowed. Rule number two: No profanity. Rule number three: No street slang.

And already I'm breaking two of the three parent-enforced rules. Standing here cavorting with the likes of a potential hoodlum and allowing the word swagger-licious—*gasp*—to enter my mind. Oh, this is grounds for a long, drawn-out lecture on how irresponsible it is to keep company with someone like Mr. Swag. And how catastrophic using such vernacular is. How unfitting it is. How improper it is. How unladylike it is. Blah, blah, blah.

Well, guess what?

I don't see anything wrong with it. Swaggerlicious. Swaggerlicious. Swag. Ger. Licious. There. I've said it.

And this guy right here reeks of it. Okay, along with the marijuana I'm sure he's smoked right before coming into the mall. I glance up at his ear and notice he has a Black & Mild cigar tucked behind it. But that's neither here nor there.

Point is, I'm tired of fitting into everyone else's box of expectations. I'm tired of being proper and polite—*all* the time. Why must I use proper English all the time? Why can't I take a leave of absence from *talking* and *sounding* white, just once?

I want a sabbatical from my life, just for the summer. Is

there anything wrong with wanting a change of pace? No.
I don't think so.

I'm sick of being everything everyone else wants, ex-
pects, me to be—*all* the time. The sixteen-year-old, college-
bound, soon-to-be junior who gets straight A's in school;
the high school varsity cheerleader who executes every
floor routine with precision; the daughter who always lis-
tens to her parents and never breaks any of their rules—
no matter how ridiculous I think most of them are; the
little sister who has had to constantly live in the shadows
of her three overprotective, overachieving, academically
and athletically gifted brothers.

"You have some sexy lips, ma. I just wanna lean in 'n'
kiss 'em."

I blink Mr. Swag back into view.

Wait.

Did he just say what I think he did?

I ask him to repeat himself. He does. "I wanna kiss you.
Word is bond."

"You don't even know me like that." I try to stay cool
about it and act like having some random guy telling me
he wants to kiss me is an everyday occurrence when it's
more like a once-in-a-lifetime opportunity that I am about
to blow.

"Yeah, but I can *get* to know you like that." He steps in
closer. "If you let me."

I am feeling light-headed. And right now. Here's my
dilemma: I've never, ever gone against my parents. I'm the
perfect daughter, the perfect friend, and the perfect little
Miss Goody Two-shoes.

In a nutshell, my life is *predictable*. And *boring*.

But, like I said already, the school year is officially over.

It's the start of the summer. And I want to have fun. I want to do something exciting. I want to live on the edge a little. Be daring. Be adventurous.

Instead of living vicariously through the characters in some of the hood—oops, I mean, urban—books I read, I want to be the girl exploring the world outside of the one my parents have given me. I want a little taste of the wild side.

A little slice of the hood pie.

Just a little.

I glance over my shoulder quickly to see if anyone's looking over at us. Then look up into his smoldering brown eyes, stepping closer into him.

One kiss won't hurt. Will it?

GREAT BOOKS,
GREAT SAVINGS!

When You Visit Our Website:
www.kensingtonbooks.com
You Can Save Money Off The Retail Price
Of Any Book You Purchase!

- **All Your Favorite Kensington Authors**
- **New Releases & Timeless Classics**
- **Overnight Shipping Available**
- **eBooks Available For Many Titles**
- **All Major Credit Cards Accepted**

Visit Us Today To Start Saving!
www.kensingtonbooks.com

All Orders Are Subject To Availability.
Shipping and Handling Charges Apply.
Offers and Prices Subject To Change Without Notice.